I0621238

EQUALITY OF SERVICE

A COLONY SERIES PARANORMAL ROMANCE

REGINA MORRIS

EQUALITY OF SERVICE

Equality of Service
[Formerly entitled "William's Tale"]
Regina Morris
Silkhaven Publishing, LLC
Smashwords Edition

Please visit author Regina Morris on her website
http://www.reginamorris.com

Join Regina Morris' mailing list for games, freebies, and
information about new releases at http://newsletter.
reginamorris.com

Regina Morris enjoys connecting with fans on social
media. Please find her at:
Facebook: http://www.facebook.com/ReginaAnnMorris
(@ReginaMorris)

Twitter: http://www.twitter.com/ReginaMorris
(@ReginaMorris)

Pinterest: http://www.pinterest.com/ReginaAnnMorris

A covert team of sexy vampires protects the President of the United States in the COLONY series of paranormal suspenseful romances.

While guarding the President at a school event, a vampire COLONY agent, William, meets the woman of his dreams —a human woman who is a teacher at the school. First impressions being what they are, he finds her sexy and opinionated, unfortunately, her dance card appears to be full and he's unsure how to woo her when he can't even take her out to dinner, without her being the meal.

Jackie discovers a hidden agenda in the President's school visit and believes William to be a mockery of the American dream of equality for all. Can a past Freedom Rider and racial activist from the 1960s, now turned vampire, prove to the love of his life that he's not a political puppet?

TEAM CODE NAME: COLONY

Council **Of** **L**egalized **O**utlanders for **N**ational securit**Y**

Silkhaven Publishing, LLC

ISBN: 978–0–9914034–4–8 (ebook)

ISBN: 978-1-948997-09-6 (paperback)

Library of Congress Control Number: 2014909132

Copyright (c) 2014-2020, Regina Morris

(V5) – January 20, 2020

This book is a work of fiction. Any references to historical events, real people, or real places are used fictitiously. All of the characters, organizations, places and events portrayed in this novel are either products of the author's imagination or are fictitiously used. Any resemblance to actual persons, living or dead, business establishments, events, or locales is entirely coincidental.

All rights reserved. No part of this book may be used or reproduced in any manner without the written permission of the author Regina Morris and the publisher Silkhaven Publishing, LLC with the exception in the case of brief quotations embodied in critical articles and reviews.

Printed in the United States of America.

Silkhaven Publishing, LLC does not have any control over and does not assume any responsibility for author or third–party Web sites or their content.

The scanning, uploading, and distribution of this book via the internet or via any other means without the permission of Silkhaven Publishing, LLC or Regina Morris is illegal and punishable by law. To obtain a copy of this novel, please purchase only through authorized electronic or print editions, and do not participate in or encourage electronic piracy of copyrighted materials.

DISCAIMERS:

This novel is for mature audiences only. Violence, sex, and nudity are described in this book and the target audience is for individuals 18+ years of age.

Even though the story takes place in and around Washington, DC, the White House, and the President of the United States, this book is a suspenseful paranormal romance which is humorously told, and not a political thriller.

❀ Created with Vellum

CONTENTS

VAMPIRES EXIST AMONG US

They can be our neighbor, best friend, our child's teacher...

They alter their aged appearance based upon the amount of blood they consume. They move to a new area, drink a lot of blood, and appear young.

Slowly they limit their intake of blood and age, right in front of our unsuspecting eyes. After decades, they fake their death, move, and do it over and over again.

Most live quiet lives in an effort to blend in.

Some, however, want power and control.
The COLONY is an elite group of vampires sworn to protect the president of the United States from these rogue vampires.

TEAM CODE NAME: COLONY

Council **O**f **L**egalized **O**utlanders for **N**ational securit**Y**

*W*illiam reread the text message from his team members, who were out of town on assignment with the President. *"POTUS lockdown. All secure."*

Security for the trip was fine with the President of the United States on lockdown. William remained thankful to have the time off from the team. Relieved actually. The small vacation gave him time to spend at home with his family, as well as some well-deserved rest.

During the President's tenures as Commander–In–Chief, he promised to visit each state in the Union. The tour had them in Oregon tonight, with the team flying back tomorrow. Every few months the President crossed off a couple of the states. Since this was his second term in office, he worked his second round of visits.

William wandered down the hallway to his children's bedrooms, trying to be as quiet as possible. His fifteen year old son, Sinclair, lay in his bed watching YouTube on his tablet. Why was Sinclair still up? His bedtime was hours ago. After William told him for the second time to go to bed, he continued down the hallway to his daughter's room.

Nicole slept soundly in her bed, her arm around her doll. William entered the room and covered the child, which caused her to moan quietly and sink into the blanket for warmth. She was twelve but still on the small-side. He caressed the girl's cheek, stroking her hair off her face, and left the room.

William's next stop was in the nursery. There his newborn baby, Hannah, quietly slept. Of the three children, Hannah seemed the most clingy, and the one most likely not to fall asleep—or stay asleep—at night. William gave a slight sigh as he smiled at the sleeping babe.

He tiptoed carefully from the room, stepping over the creaking floorboard that always seemed to wake Hannah up. He made his way to the kitchen where his wife, Jackie, and another team member, Alex, sat at the table. Brown fabric was draped over Jackie's lap, a pin cushion strapped to her wrist, and the hum of a sewing machine came to an abrupt stop as she looked at her husband.

"They all asleep?"

He shrugged and took a seat between her and Alex. "Not all, but enough of them," he said half jokingly.

"What does that mean?" Alex asked as she sipped her wine.

William looked at the newest member of the COLONY. Alex had been nominated as the team's new COLONY Director, but she had declined the position since she had fallen in love with their coven master, Raymond. Raymond later turned her so she could work alongside the team.

"He means the most important one, baby Hannah, is asleep." Jackie stretched in her seat, her spine cracking as her muscles flexed. "I nursed her twice and rocked her for thirty minutes before you came over."

"She doesn't go down easily," William agreed. "When she is up, the whole house is up."

Gathering the material from her lap, Jackie piled it neatly on the table. "Thanks for helping us make these costumes for the Thanksgiving play at Nicole's school."

"Not at all," Alex said as she grabbed some beads and followed William's lead of threading them on a thin strip of fabric with a knot on one end. "What types of costumes are you making?"

William compared his recently made bead string with the others on the table. Realizing it was shorter than the rest, he grabbed another two beads. "Nicole is a squaw in the production. Jackie got roped into making ten Native American costumes for the play."

"*I volunteered*," Jackie said, smiling, her fangs slightly showing. "*You* were roped in by me."

Alex began a second strand of beads and watched as Jackie sewed some that William had made earlier onto one of the costumes. The Singer danced expertly under Jackie's hand.

"Did you have a pattern?" Alex asked.

Jackie chuckled. "White pillow cases dyed brown, with slits for the head and arms, and beads sewn on isn't exactly a challenging project." She picked up a finished costume and pointed to the different features. "I even added a couple of darts in the back to give it some shape as well as cut the bottom to make fringe."

William placed another completed bead strand on the

table. "I have no idea what a dart is, but it is very clever, babe."

Alex turned a costume over and pointed to the two sewn gatherings in back. "Darts." She then placed it back down on the table and looked around. "Are they going to wear feathered headdresses?"

Jackie's eyes lit up. "I almost forgot." She walked to the countertop nearest the stove and plugged in a hot glue gun. Pointing to a bag of feathers, she added, "We've got everything we need."

"I'm on it." William stood and manned the glue gun.

Alex smiled as she looked from one to another, then she took another sip of wine. "You two make a cute couple. I never heard the story of how you met."

Both William and Jackie snickered.

"What?" Alex asked.

Jackie gave her a wry smile. "Within five minutes of meeting the man, I was yelling at him and calling him a mockery of the American dream of equality for all."

William let out a slight chuckle. "She had no idea I was a Freedom Rider from the 1960s who died in the pursuit of equality, and who was turned into a vampire."

Alex's jaw dropped. "No way!"

"Girl, I was awful to him. And, I had no idea vampires existed." Jackie walked over to William, her arms wrapping around her man as she hugged him. "I said he had forged a system of lies for the American people and was spoon–feeding it to them." She halfway laughed and looked her husband in the eyes. "And you know what? You ate my nasty attitude up and knew I was the woman of your dreams!"

"Woman, you were so smitten with me that you couldn't keep your hands off."

Alex sat back in her chair, no longer stringing beads. "Tell me the whole story."

Jackie looked up at William, whose response was to shrug. "Go ahead and tell it your way, babe. I'll jump in when needed."

Jackie took a deep breath as she returned to the kitchen table. "Well, our story began on a cold spring day..."

*a*n entire relationship and three beautiful children earlier…

Jackie's body ached, and all she wanted was a hot bath. She opened the door to her apartment complex and left the bitter cold of the Maryland winter outside. She dusted off her jacket, removed her gloves, and loosened the scarf around her neck. Just a few steps into the lobby of the building and she already felt too hot to need her coat.

Her boots clicked as she crossed the tiled floor to the community mailboxes. After watching the mail tumble out once she opened the tiny door, she cursed herself for not having the post office hold it for her.

However, she was only gone a week.

An exhausting week.

She quickly scanned the mail. Why was she still getting letters address to her ex-boyfriend, Steve? She had told that man to have the post office change his address. What did she have to do? Fill out the forms for him? She grabbed a pen from her purse and crossed out her address, writing, "Forward" onto each envelope. Next time, she wasn't going to be as kind.

But she had said that to herself the last time she had checked the mail. And the time before that.

No. Not anymore. She grabbed the letters and, pressing down firmly with the pen, wrote, "Address Unknown" across the top, scratching out her earlier marks. She then slipped the letters into the outgoing mail slot. She was done playing nice with that man, and she breathed a sigh of relief. It felt good to no longer be his doormat.

She removed her coat and draped the garment over her arm. Gathering up the remaining mail, mostly bills, she carried her small suitcase up the main staircase to her apartment. Eclectic styles of artwork hung in the hallways. Not her taste, but the paintings, the plush carpet, and the light fixtures on the walls always reminded her of a library—a nice, clean library. She fumbled for her keys as she approached her door. It wasn't very late, but evidently she had made enough noise that her elderly neighbor had come out of her apartment to see who stood in the hallway.

"Oh, Jackie dear. It's you."

Jackie took a deep breath. Why couldn't she walk into her apartment without a news announcement or gossip call from Mrs. Cunningham? She was a sweet woman, although a bit eccentric and long winded. Tonight the woman wore a red housecoat, fluffy white house shoes, and her hair was curled in rollers. "Hello, Mrs. C."

"It's good to see you, Jackie. You look so nice." She touched the brim of her glasses as though getting a good look at her.

Jackie gave a wry smile. Really? She looked nice? She wore torn jeans and a dirty T-shirt. Her hair lay tied back in a kerchief, and she wore no makeup. She wasn't looking like the belle of the ball since she had spent the day moving heavy boxes. She still smiled and accepted the compliment.

"How is your father, dear?"

Leave it up to Mrs. C. to hit her with that loaded question this late at night. "As best as can be expected." Jackie slid her key into the lock of her door and heard the tumbler unlock the chamber.

"Is he all moved in?"

How the little old bitty could keep track of everyone else's whereabouts and comings and goings was beyond Jackie. She smiled at the woman as she opened the door. "Yes. He's just down the road at Silver Estates."

"That's a nice retirement home. Nancy down the hall mentioned to me that she needs to find a place for her elderly mother. Of course," Mrs. C now looked down the hallway and continued in a whisper, "she needs to find a place that is not too close to where her father lives because…"

Jackie's hand rose to stop her. "It's rather late, Mrs. C."

Her eyebrow rose, perhaps in frustration. Regardless, she kept talking. "I figured you'd be gone until at least this weekend."

It was only Thursday and Jackie had planned to take her father shopping over the next few days to buy whatever he may need for his new apartment. "Things went smoother than planned," she said.

Mrs. C's eyes lit up. "Oh, I almost forgot. You got some flowers while you were away. Caroline down the hallway got some too, but they weren't nearly as nice as yours. Hold on…" She entered her apartment and returned holding a vase of not so fresh roses. "They arrived just after you left."

Jackie quickly grabbed the flowers since they looked heavy in the old woman's arms. "Thanks Mrs. C. I appreciate you signing for them."

She offered Jackie a wide grin. "I know this is your year for getting a ring on that hand of yours. You know, you're the only single woman still on this floor."

Jackie shifted her stance to her other foot, partly because of the weight of the flowers and partly because she still carried her mail and coat. Jackie wanted to be married and perhaps have children, but she doubted that this was her year for it. She certainly didn't need to know that she was the resident spinster. "Steve and I broke up weeks ago," she explained under her breath.

Mrs. C. shook her head. "Oh, not him dear. Someone better."

Jackie bit her tongue. "Okay, if you say so. It's rather late, and I have some unpacking to do."

"If you ever need anything…"

Jackie smiled. "I know you're only across the hall." She entered her apartment, closing the door on the very sweet, but very nosey, woman.

Now alone, she studied the nearly dead flowers. She had spent an entire week moving her father into a retirement home. Well, him and his two cats. Four months had passed since her mother died from ovarian cancer, and her parents had lived out in California. Moving to Maryland was a big move for her father. At the very least, he was sensible about it. He appreciated her efforts and now only lived a few miles away.

The dead flowers went straight into the trash, but she pulled the card. Jackie took a deep breath as she read it. She prayed the flowers weren't from her ex-boyfriend. Although she didn't know who else the bouquet could have been from.

Unfortunately, the flowers were Steve's second attempt to woo her back. She ripped up the card and threw it in the trash. There was no way she was allowing that cheating bastard back into her life. She wanted a man to share his life with her. To be with her all the way until death did them part—just like her father had been there for her mother. The two of them had a great love story.

Tears welled up in her eyes. She missed her mom and had hated to see the pain in her father's eyes over the last year as his wife slowly withered away. People should live forever, or at the very least not die such lingering deaths.

"Buck up, Jackie," she thought to herself. She was lucky to have had her mother in her life as long as she had, and luckier still to have her father. Her parents did love each other. Love stories like theirs didn't exist anymore. Which is why she planned to swear off men forever... or at least until Mr. Right came into her life.

Her shoulders sank and she let out all the air in her lungs. She had lived with three men, and none of them were the love of her life. Hell, she probably wouldn't even recognize Mr. Right if he did come by.

Just then, Jackie's phone rang.

William scratched his arm again. The wool suit created a rash on his skin. He cursed at the cold chill of the brisk morning air as he and another COLONY agent, Ben, drove to Criswell Elementary school. March had come in like a lion with its blustery winds and low chill factors. He couldn't wait for the month to exit like a lamb.

What bothered William the most was the fact that he didn't even need the warmth of the wool suit, or the full-length, lined winter coat he wore. Posing as human proved to be a pain at times. Honestly, he could be out in shorts and feel fine. But today he felt like a dressed up monkey. Dark suit, red silk tie, dress shoes, and, of course, the sunglasses. He hated it all. A pair of jeans and a comfortable T-shirt were more his style. Actually, an Afro was also more to his liking. But since he worked with the covert vampire team protecting the President, he kept his hair short and professional, and he sported no facial hair.

Looking out of the car window, William took in the stately neighborhood they drove through. Solid brick two-story houses, fireplaces, expensive cars in the drive-ways… everything appeared polished, all the way down to the non-cracked sidewalks. Certainly, no gangs traveled these streets, and he bet the only person of color would be a maid.

"Are you sure this is the right address?" he asked Ben.

"Brighton Corbe Estates. Essex Avenue. Should be around the corner." Ben handed the map to William. "Don't even suggest I ask for directions."

William took the map and barely glanced at it. Ben had worked with the COLONY decades longer than William. Ben was one of the founding members of the team, which formed after the assassination of Abraham Lincoln.

Another turn and a short drive down the street led them to the elementary school. The large building stood tall on its large lot. It was all white brick, and had a spacious courtyard, and offered plenty of parking.

"Let me get this straight," he said, challenging Ben. "The President has taken a lot of flack for not caring enough about our education system, and especially for not providing for underprivileged kids." William pointed at the building. "Does he think this sanctuary with no broken windows and no kids on state funded lunch programs will really fit the bill?"

Ben parked the car in front of the school. "I only have to protect the man. I don't have to agree with him."

"But doesn't it bother you?"

Ben glared at William. "Change takes its sweet time. You're not that old, but you can remember the riots of the '60s—the inequality we suffered. I've seen a lot of change. Don't forget, our people weren't even allowed an education when I was a boy."

William felt a pang of guilt. Ben had been born a slave in the 1800s. Surely he had seen worse discrimination in his days than William had. Ben stood the tallest and largest of all the COLONY vamps. Looking like a linebacker in corporate dress, William could only imagine the life Ben had been forced to live back in the days of slavery.

The two exited the car and did a surveillance sweep of the outside of the building. "No security cameras," Ben said. "The human Secret Service agents already noted that. There will be some in place by Monday morning when the big man arrives."

When they easily entered the building, William rolled

his eyes. "Outdated metal detectors. Only one manual security check. I wish the old man were visiting a museum or library. Schools are so open."

"Schools are getting more and more secure, but some are behind the times." Ben led William down the short corridor to the main office. Before they entered, he whispered, "The human team already has a plan to better secure the building. We just have to visit with the staff and make sure no vampires are around."

CHAPTER 2

On Monday, Jackie drove in to work. As a substitute teacher, she always tried to arrive early. Different streets, different traffic... she never wanted to be late, even if she hated the school.

Criswell Elementary ranked as a top notch school across the state. Of course, in an abundantly rich neighborhood, that would be expected.

As she turned onto the street to the school, she was surprised to find a group of policemen waving her into a secured roped–off parking lot. After showing her ID and explaining that she was subbing for a teacher, she was allowed to park. The officers gave her no explanation for the parking precautions, but since she saw men on nearby rooftops, possibly snipers, she assumed maybe the President was nearby.

The policemen asked her to exit the car while they searched the interior, the underside, and the trunk for explosives and weapons. They didn't say that was what they looked for, but it seemed obvious to Jackie.

She felt a momentary gush of excitement. After all, she had never seen a President before. But over the years she lived in the D.C. area, the reality was that presidential outtings were more of a hassle than anything else. Her car's strip search was proof of that this morning.

She checked her watch. It was still early, but not as early as she would have preferred. With the possibility of the President nearby, it now made sense that many of the streets in the neighborhood that were blocked off, and the detours, although short, had caused her to zigzag around in a maze–like fashion—adding more time to her morning commute.

She smiled politely to the officers as they completed their task and instructed her to collect her belongings and go directly to the school on the marked path where they could monitor her. She gathered her purse from her Ford Pinto and felt her anger build. Not because of the lost time, but for the fact that she was subbing at a school that oozed money from every hallway. She actually enjoyed working at a school with the newer textbooks, the computer centers, and the low student–to–teacher ratio. Those things were always nice. But they reminded her of the schools of her past where she taught from outdated textbooks, where no one had a computer, and where the classrooms were filled with students—if the kids didn't stay home caring for younger siblings, or even worse, their own babies.

No. She refused to revisit that frustration. She was an educator. She taught children, and it didn't matter where she taught as long as children learned. Plus, it shouldn't matter if the children were privileged here, that they lived in an affluent neighborhood where most families had both parents. The fact that her school had lost funding and had to let her go... Well, that was unfortunate. Even with her protests and petition, she still lost her job. But such was life.

She straightened her skirt and buttoned her coat. She just wanted the day to be over with. The call had come in late the other night with a need for a substitute teacher. She thought back to the call. It had not come from her usual dispatcher, but from a man claiming to be from a different department. Either way, she didn't recognize the phone number but did appreciate more than a day's notice that she would be needed. After all, a job was a job.

She quickly walked down the path to the school, realizing that the President may be visiting the building at some point today. Again she felt a chill up her spine as some excitement built, but what were the odds she'd actually see the man?

The school's side entrance was barricaded by a row of wooden sawhorses, with a handsome man standing guard. A cool breeze blew down on her violently, causing her to run towards the main entrance. She took in a deep breath when she reached the doors and looked back to study the man who was dressed in a suit and tie. He certainly was eye catching. Strong jaw, muscular build, and a certain kindness in his face. Jackie bit her lip. If he's a teacher, he's a well dressed one. He didn't even look cold standing outside. He just looked sexy. Perhaps she'd have a chance to meet him later in the day.

Then again, he could be Secret Service. They wore suits, black suits with dark sunglasses—or so she thought.

The man glanced her way and she felt the heat of his stare. His sexy gaze was enticing, but no. She looked away, remembering she had promised herself no more men—not even handsome godlike visions like him. Her plan was to give all men up until she found Mr. Right. A handsome man like this was probably a player. She didn't need the baggage, or the drama.

She entered the building and a gust of wind caught the door, forcing it from her hand. She pulled the door shut and enjoyed the warmth she found inside the building. She had only subbed at this school once before, and the place was as nice as she remembered. It felt like entering Shangri-la. The teachers wore suits and no trash lay piled up in the hallway. Not only did the school cafeteria serve delicious meals, but it also had an expensive cappuccino machine. Yes, it was the type of place that could spoil you. She didn't even worry about wearing her good jewelry to this school—not that she had any expensive pieces, but nice costume ones. Today she wore a teal, two-piece skirt set with matching pumps. The suit was one of her favorite outfits, and considering what the teacher, or perhaps Secret Service agent, at the side door was wearing, she was glad to have dressed up.

Making her way to the office, she wasn't surprised to see an armed guard carrying a metal detector wand. The entire hallway had been blocked off, making the only entrance into the school through the main office and it's side door that led into the hallway to the library. The female guard waved her over and instructed her to place her bags on the table. Next, Jackie lifted her arms and the wand traveled across her body, quietly humming as it scanned her for any weapons. Once her bags were checked, Jackie showed her ID, signed in, and was instructed to go to the library.

Jackie was now certain. The President was coming.

CHAPTER 3

*J*ackie tried to catch her breath, but found the task too overwhelming. The President. Here. Just moments away. It seemed almost too much to take in. But, if what everyone was saying proved to be true, the man would be here soon.

What a day to be sub at a school! From what Jackie could tell, none of the staff was informed ahead of time. Based upon the panicked expression on the principal's face, Jackie even doubted the principal knew of the President's arrival. Though he may have just been nervous.

Jackie didn't particularly approve of this President. Heck, she hadn't even voted for the man. But she was about to meet the most powerful man in the free world. She now felt butterflies in her stomach and swallowed the lump growing in her throat. She couldn't wait to share this with her father later.

She stood in the library with a dozen teachers and school staff huddled in one corner. From her last subbing job at this school, she knew more teachers worked here than were accounted for in the library. She figured the numbers had been kept small for security reasons, which made her feel doubly blessed to have been selected to meet the man.

Her gaze darted to the four men in black suits, each with a com unit in their ears standing formidably at the exits. Were they Secret Service? Maybe NSA or CIA. Whatever the case, the situation fascinated her.

A fifth agent led some children into the room one by one and arranged them in a circle on the floor. At the center of the circle sat a large wooden chair—obviously for the big man himself whenever he arrived.

Jackie took a deep breath. School was about to begin, and she had not made her way to her appointed classroom. How would she be able to tell which children were her responsibility for the day? She knew she subbed for a second grade class, but wasn't sure what to do next. Fortunately, she didn't have to decide on her own. A Secret Service agent waved her over and told her where to stand since she had been selected to shake the President's hand.

Her heart skipped a beat. *"Shake his hand?"* she thought as the biggest smile crossed her face. Hell, yeah! She definitely wanted to do that.

She stood away from the circle and the wooden chair, but close to the library door itself. She wished she could be closer to where the President would be sitting, but wasn't about to complain since she would get her own moment with the man. Regardless, she still had a good view of where he would be sitting from this angle. She just hoped she wouldn't be too nervous when he approached her.

Ok, now her hands began to sweat, and she realized she was holding her breath. She dug her fingernails into the palm of her hands. Come on, girl. Get it together. He's a man like everyone else. He probably does this stuff all the time.

Maybe.

Something felt eerie to her. The agent who had brought the kids in took a post near the door and seemed to have stopped fetching more children. Another agent, who stood impressively tall and had the build of a line-backer, now approached the circle of kids. He looked from one child to the other, as though memorizing their faces. All in all, about thirty kids sat on the floor. All remained quiet.

The amount of children wasn't the school's complete complement, but not all of them would fit in the library of course. Perhaps the President would walk from classroom to classroom later. All the children, as well as the teachers, deserved a chance to meet the man.

Wait a minute. Jackie scanned the circle of children. Over half of them were children of color, with the white children sitting the farthest from where the President would be seated. Normally, not an odd sight, but this school must be at least ninety percent white, making most of the children on the floor a subpopulation of the school, with fewer than ten percent representation.

Yes, the subpopulations were all *well* represented on *that* floor.

Very well represented, indeed.

She studied the agent towering over them—a tall African–American man, perhaps in his fifties. A Hispanic agent had led the children into the room. And, of course, there was the female agent who ran the metal detector. She appeared to be Asian. The only white agent had been the blond man who told her where to stand.

Yeah, the token white-boy in the room.

Jackie didn't know the percentage of diversity for the Secret Service, but this room certainly seemed stacked to favor minorities. With perception being reality, she began putting two-and-two together. The President needed to appear in favor of education, as well as minority issues. She rolled her eyes. Standing there, she wasn't part of the solution—she was a part of the problem!

Chatter came from the hallway, and then two more agents entered with members of the press. The press then positioned themselves around the room for the best camera angles. One reporter stood close to Jackie and did a sound check for her cameraman.

Her jaw tightened. How dare they use her in such a ruse.

The Secret Service must have rounded up every child matching a certain criterion and hauled them into the library so the President could put on a show for the press. Her cheeks flushed as she grew angrier at the possibility that she may be right. How come no one in the press saw through this hoax?

Well, she had seen through it. When the President walked through the door, she wasn't going to play the puppet in his show. She would give him a piece of her mind. As she waited for the President to arrive, she mentally rehearsed what she planned to say to the man. She wanted to be firm with him and to point out to the press the obvious game he was playing.

And then the moment arrived. Her hands balled into

fists, her eyes focused on the door, and her breathing became even. She was determined to be a force to be reckoned with, and he would rue the day he messed with the education system and underprivileged kids.

More noise came from the hallway, and when the door opened, Jackie felt the wind beneath her wings disappear and her anger leave her body. Her muscles relaxed and she felt her legs go weak as noodles. The man who stood guard outside the school, the most gorgeous man she had ever laid eyes on, had walked through that door. Damn. He looked good.

He stood a good six feet in height, had ebony skin like hers, with piercing brown eyes that appeared soulful and kind. His suit, not black, but a darker gray, fit him well. It made him look powerful and in charge. She watched as he spoke into a com unit, perhaps giving orders to the other agents standing nearby.

Taking a deep breath, she thought he was the most beautiful man in the world. She had even forgotten the President was coming for a visit.

With the press corps already escorted into the library, William now walked ahead of the President to get him safely into position. At first glance, William confirmed what Ben had already told him through the com units— no vampires were in the room and a human agent named Juan had positioned the children, with Ben now guarding their moods. Everything was a go.

It surprised William how quietly the group of children sat on the floor. Ben had a special gift. Not all vampires had one, and William was one vampire to prove the rule. Ben could read the auras of humans and vampires. He could even alter the mood of humans, which was evident by the angelic children circling the wooden chair.

The President walked behind William and two other agents. Another three agents followed him. The first step on the tour was to shake hands with a teacher at the school. If the plan remained intact, that teacher would be standing just to his left.

William's eyes wandered in the appointed direction. It was her. The beautiful woman from outside earlier that day. His job this morning was to carefully watch everyone who left the blocked off parking area and walked towards the school, confirming they were not a vampire. He had noticed her immediately. She was a curvy human woman, standing at an average height—gorgeous, with a smile which could light up heaven. Her bluish-green suit gave her a well polished, professional appearance, and her simple jewelry complemented her dark wavy, shoulder length hair. She appeared as a vision of loveliness.

The President nearly crashed into William, so he stepped aside and allowed the President to continue his journey to the designated spot. A man, whom William assumed to be the principal, joined them. Polite, cordial words were exchanged, and a photographer leaned in and took a picture of the President shaking not just the principal's hand, but also the teacher's hand as he made his way into the room.

It wasn't as though William focused on any of the pleasantries. He had stood security for the President plenty of times in the past, and had learned to focus on merely security issues. But then, he heard something,

something liltingly beautiful. It was the beautiful woman's laugh. He focused on her gracious smile, not knowing what the President had said to make her so joyful. William found himself smiling back to her, although he remained cautious not to show his fangs.

The most important piece of information William gathered from the photo op was the angel's name—Jackie Pearlman.

It became a name now permanently etched into his memory.

CHAPTER 4

*D*ry, chapped hands.

The President's dire need of hand lotion surprised Jackie. She sighed heavily as she followed the man with her gaze. The handsome agent led the President through the library to the crowd of children waiting for him.

She had planned to tell the President he had no right to create this charade. She figured she couldn't outright yell at the man, but a knowing smile and a whispered, "I know what you're doing," would have been subtle enough to please her.

But no. She grinned like an idiot from ear to ear and even laughed when he made a joke about needing to be extra quiet since they were in the library.

A backbone. She wished she had one.

Watching the President talk with the children made her skin crawl. He smiled, he laughed, he even talked with them. But as he looked in their eyes, did he understand what the kids were saying? What they needed? What they hoped their future would be like?

Now needing an antacid, she realized she needed to change her attitude. For the most part, second and third graders found it thrilling to be meeting the President, and they had every right to meet the man who had neglected equal rights in their country. Oh, the man wasn't racist—at least not overtly so. But he had canceled many bills which would have supported inner–city funding for schools, rec centers, and even planned parenthood facilities. Naturally, his religious upbringing gave him concerns over the latter one. No need to help children who were sixteen and already had baby–daddys and baby–mamas in their lives. Or, *not* in their lives as was usually the case.

Jackie unclenched her hands, which had balled into fists. She tried to shake off her pending rage, but it proved hard to do as she watched the President talking to the future generation of America.

William stood at attention, but couldn't take his eyes off Jackie. He watched as her chest rose and fell with each breath she took, how often her eyes blinked, and he noticed she wore no ring on her finger, which was always a good sign. He liked the fire he saw in her eyes. She embodied sexiness, in a pissed off, please–me–now sort of way.

He bit his lip as his gaze traveled from her dark hair and flushed cheeks to her full bosom. Her outfit, although conservative, did have a slight, plunging neckline which showed off her cleavage.

Staying on course, his gaze wandered down to her legs. The woman had legs 'til Tuesday. From his current location, he couldn't see how firm her bottom was but suspected she was blessed in all the right areas.

Yes. She was near perfection. The type of woman he had searched decades for. William's body now tingled with excitement. He closed his eyes and pressed his lips firmly against his extended fangs.

Oh God. Not here. Not now.

Sporting an erection in front of children, and on camera, was not putting his best foot forward. His pants became tighter with his length hardened, so he subtly confirmed his suit jacket was buttoned in front to provide some protection.

He took a deep breath and focused on his job and on the President. Honestly, looking at the old man was like splashing cold water on his libido. Nothing was sexy about a sixty-three year old man pretending to laugh with children he probably didn't care anything about.

Of course, the press went crazy. Cameras snapped pictures left and right. Pictures that now, thanks to the digital age, would show crisp and sharp images of both him and Ben. William had turned his head so he would not face the cameras head-on, which proved difficult since the press stood everywhere. He noticed Ben looking directly at the kids, obviously still controlling their behavior and moods. Every once in a while, Ben would scan the room, but his focus remained clearly on the kids.

That's why it surprised him to hear Ben's voice over the ear bud com unit. In a high pitch only vampires and dogs could hear, Ben said, "We may have a problem. Lady in a greenish-colored dress. Her aura shows she is extremely upset."

None of the other agents had heard Ben's remarks. They were all human and their ears couldn't register the high pitch. William looked around for a woman in such a colored dress, but he wasn't sure if Ben meant the teal one worn by Jackie. He followed Ben's stare so he could find her.

Why was Ben staring right at Jackie? The problem couldn't have been with her, could it? William asked in the same high pitch, "The teacher the President shook hands with?"

When Ben acknowledged that was whom he had meant, he instructed William to remove the woman from the room.

A cold chill ran up William's spine and his stomach felt queasy. He hoped there was some type of mistake. Of course, he was happy to have a reason to talk with the woman, but could she mean to do the President harm? Without giving too much thought to the task, he snapped into presidential protection mode. He approached the woman, touched her arm, and then whispered, "Ma'am, please come with me."

Her deep brown eyes looked into his, and he heard a slight gasp from her. Her eyebrows raised questioningly, but he firmly escorted her from the room without another word.

CHAPTER 5

*W*illiam lightly gripped the crux of Jackie's arm. She seemed startled at first, and her heels gave her a moment's pause as he led her out of the room, but overall, she easily followed.

Standing in the hallway, William glanced down the right corridor leading to the principal's office. Damn. Too many humans were milling about. Looking to his left, he saw a hallway running past the security station. No one stood around that area, so he walked Jackie down that way.

The security guard proved to be the only obstacle, but not for long. William's eyes locked onto hers as she stood. "You will let us pass." Her eyes dimmed, and her skin instantly paled. She scooted out of their way and paid them no mind.

A door in the hallway with the word "Nurse" across the frosted, cracked window caught his attention. The unlocked door easily opened, so he led Jackie inside. Now alone, the two were out of earshot of any other human.

He heard Jackie's heart beating loudly with his sensitive vampire ears as he closed the door behind them. Her eyes widened with fright as she stared at the door.

"You need to unhand me." She twisted her arm and forced him to let go. He had barely held it, afraid he may too easily bruise her—or break her arm since his vampire strength sometimes did get the better of him when dealing with humans.

Her body stood tense; at her full height she was only standing past his shoulders. He listened as she took a deep breath and looked him over questioningly.

"Well?" she asked. "You dragged me here for a reason. So spill it," she said, biting her lower lip and shifting from one foot to the other.

She seemed so angry. Her cheeks were flushed with blood, and she had such a defiant expression on her face. He liked opinionated, strong women, and she looked lovely to him. But she was obviously hiding something.

He took a deep breath as he eyed her. Even with her small, human form, she appeared to be a force to be reckoned with. She seemed to be the type of woman that prison inmates would say Ma'am to instead of making catcalls. God, if she could, he'd bet she would belt him across the face if he got out of line. He found the notion incredibly sexy.

"Now don't be starin' at me like that. I'm guessing this is about my petition," she said, standing her ground. "I got more than the required number of names for it, and those schools need their funding back. I was only kidding when I wrote to my congressmen saying he needed to stop pretending to protect us citizens." She paused. "I know I shouldn't have said he's just sittin' around on his fat ass while inner–city kids do without, but the man *is* in office to hear the needs of his constituents. And if he ain't up to the task…"

William held out his hand to stop her. For as well–bred as she appeared, she had an inner–city accent—a real 'life on the street' way about her that he assumed came out when she was angry. "A petition isn't why I removed you from the library."

Her eyes widened, and he noticed her pause for a moment. Then she regrouped with fury. "You have no right to haul me out of that room like a common criminal —and in front of the principal and the teachers."

"Ma'am, you need to settle down." He wasn't sure if it was her tone, or the fact that her finger was wagging at him like he was a naughty boy, but he felt like she was in control of the room. He figured she took control in any room she was in. She certainly qualified as a spitfire.

Giving him a stern glance, she rubbed her arm where he had held her. "Do you know how hard you grabbed me?"

For the first time, William noticed how muscular the woman was. He had felt it when he had touched her, but it hadn't registered. When she had pulled away, she had *really* pulled away. He wasn't holding her with all his might, but he surely left a bruise.

He gave her an unresponsive glance and got to the business at hand. "I'm sorry for any inconvenience, but I need to ask you about your intentions involving the President."

"My intentions?"

He looked deeply into her soulful brown eyes, and compelled her to answer his questions truthfully. Her eyes went dim and lost their spark. Her skin paled, and she became under his power—like a doll he controlled.

William glanced away. He hated seeing humans in this state. Mere human puppets. It never bothered him when a criminal was under a compulsion, or even a member of the wait staff so they'd not notice him acting un–human-like. But to see a beautiful, passionate woman like this go spiritless, it was difficult to look her in the eyes afterward.

And she was beautiful. A phrase that came quickly to his mind was, "strikingly put together." Her fingers flaunted a manicure, and he suspected her boot–covered toes sported a nice pedicure as well. Her thick shoulder-length modern hairdo seemed stylish, although he didn't keep up with fashion trends. All of her jewelry was simple, but coordinated with her outfit. Even her tight, well fitting suit showed off her shapely figure and complemented her warm mocha skin tone.

In the state of compulsion she was in, she would just stand there waiting for him to ask his questions, so he didn't keep her waiting.

"Are you angry or upset with the President or his administration?"

"Yes, I am."

What? That wasn't what he had hoped to hear, especially how quickly she had responded. He carefully phrased his next question. "Do you intend to do any harm to the President?"

"Harm? Don't be silly."

He looked into her eyes. Normally, humans answered sparsely with an even tone while being compelled. Her responses seemed ripe with attitude. She remained compelled, and her sassy demeanor impressed him.

He undid the compulsion, while compelling her to forget she had ever been compelled. Then, following protocol, he planned to detain her for the remainder of the President's stay.

"Why were you angry when you saw the President?"

It was as if he'd opened a can of worms. Jackie shared her concerns with the current administration, childhood education, and the way minorities were being treated in the workforce. Overall, she gave a verbal tongue lashing to the current administration.

"I just wish I had said it to the President himself," Jackie said as she took a few steps around the room. "Instead, I only smiled, laughed at his joke, and let him walk right on by."

And that's when William pinpointed the source of her anger. "So, you're upset with yourself?"

Her hand extended as she turned back around to face him. "Don't get me started."

William leaned against the nurse's desk and studied Jackie as she continued voicing her concerns. She was so passionate about her job and about teaching. He could tell the kids she taught meant everything to her. He'd had no idea teachers taught curriculum towards certain state and national testing—that their job had been reduced to seeing how many kids could pass certain tests, regardless whether the teacher could reach them or not. The facts about subpopulations and testing within the schools fascinated him, as did the ways in which schools got ranked. A ranking that affected a school's budget within each district. It was a whole new world to William.

He allowed her to rant a bit about the school district. He realized she had picked up on the same racial concerns he had when he first laid eyes on this school. The selection of a beautiful building in the middle of rich suburbia, a far cry from one of the poorest school districts, seemed a bit contradictory to the selection of students and teachers assembled to meet the President. Regardless of whether the President had chosen this school for safety, or for a another reason, he couldn't allow her to continue to believe her allegations.

"The President isn't here on any ruse to increase his popularity with minorities," William said, doing his job.

Her eyes narrowed and a scowl appeared on her face. "Of course *you'd* say that. You're a mockery of equality in this country."

His jaw nearly hit the floor. *He was a mockery?* He had lived through the heart of the equal rights campaigns of the 1960s and had fought —and died— for equality for all. Jackie had spent less than five minutes with him. She had no right to jump to such conclusions. "Explain."

She looked at him and explained the racial distribution of not just the kids in the library, but also with the agents on duty near the President. William himself, with his dark colored skin, being one of the problems.

William glanced down at his dark skin. He had felt awkward about this entire school setup, and he thought, perhaps, he might be one of the problems. Regardless, he needed to have her believe the school, and the children, were picked at random. "Juan, the agent who brought the kids into the library, is a friend of mine," he lied. He had met the man once or twice, but really had kept his distance since Juan was a human agent. "I assure you, his selection was random," he added for good measure.

It was a stock answer, and William hated saying it. Oh

sure, the diversity of the selected kids was fabulous, but it felt wrong. The selection went against the odds and it ate at him—not just the selection process, but lying to her. Still, he added, "Please believe me the selection of kids was not a calculated result of a President hoping to seem compassionate towards minorities."

"Compassionate?" She rolled her eyes at the very idea.

"I also know the other agents on duty today." Overall, there were three COLONY vamps present (him, Ben and another agent, Sterling, who had led the reporters in) and a dozen secret service men. "The agents are on duty because it's their day to be in the President's inner loop of protection. No one stacked minorities in the Secret Service for this trip today." At least, he hoped that to be the case. He hadn't thought about the makeup of the Secret Service staff until just this minute.

William focused his eyes on Jackie. Today was supposed to be his day off, and he did find it odd that he was asked to work the school visit. His brow furrowed as he considered the possibility that he may have been slacking in his support of equality for all. He had a cushy job on Capital Hill. He hadn't touched base with his roots in decades, and the thought saddened him. He had been a child of the system, bouncing from one foster care parent to the next. That is, until a woman he always affection-ately referred to as Mama Jackson had taken him in. She too was a spitfire who taught him to stand up for what he believed in.

He gazed into Jackie's eyes. "What else makes this visit choreographed in your eyes?"

"Out of all the teachers, *I* was selected to shake hands with the man. I mean, of all people…"

"And why would you be…"

"Now do I look like I'm done talking?" She gave him a frustrated expression, which made him wonder if he should compel her to be a bit more submissive, but he enjoyed her passion as a strong-minded individual. He looked deeply into her eyes and thought she had the same spirit as Mama Jackson, or even Rosa Parks, the woman who had refused to give up her seat on that bus so long ago.

William suspected Jackie would have marched with Dr. Martin Luther King Jr. back in the day. Changes can be made by just one person at the right time with the right fight.

Jackie blew out an exasperated sigh. "I'm sorry." Her tone sounded quieter, which surprised him. "It's not your fault I got laid off. I shouldn't take my problems out on you. Your boss, or at least the government he runs, made the budget cuts, not you."

William's eyebrow rose. She appeared honestly apologetic and regretful, even with the sarcastic remark about the President. "Don't you work here?"

Her big brown eyes gazed into his. "No. I got a call to sub. The odd thing was the call didn't come through the usual channels, but there have been so many district changes it's hard to tell."

"To tell what?"

She shook her head. "You probably can't say anything. So never mind."

He softened his stance and shifted from one foot to the other. He wasn't sure what she was talking about. "I can't say what?"

Her eyebrows furrowed. "Come on now. Doesn't me coming in to sub seem a bit... *staged?*"

The nagging feeling in the pit of his stomach grew. He had felt uneasy about this entire trip. Whatever was going on, she had sensed it as well.

Jackie shook her head. "I have it all wrapped up in my head that I was called in to sub so I could up the minority numbers. I figure that was why I had been chosen to shake the President's hand."

He cleared his throat. "*That's* not why you were chosen." He watched as she gave him a questioning glance. It was time to come clean. "*I* chose you for that position."

Before she could ask why, he held up his hand to the com unit in his ear. The agents were completing their tasks. "The President will be leaving shortly. If you ever need any help, or if you just want to talk," he said, reaching into his pocket and then putting a business card into her hand, "call me."

Jackie glanced down at the card, and he could have sworn he saw a slight smile from her.

The team was preparing for the President's departure, and William had no time to chat with Jackie since he needed to get into position. The President would be exiting from a back door of the school, near the cafeteria dumpsters. Two Presidential limos waited, one for the man himself and the other a decoy. Overall, it didn't matter which car the President left in. After all, the man visiting the school today wasn't really the President.

CHAPTER 6

*T*he team had safely escorted the presidential stand-in back to the White House, where COLONY team members divided into their respective tasks and went to work. At all times a vampire stood guard near the real President, which would have meant more COLONY members present at the school, but due to last minute security concerns, the President's decoy had been called in instead. Several other the team members watched the house from monitors and by walking the White House grounds. Vampires always sensed other predators nearby, an ability that had proven helpful many times in the past.

It would be so much easier if the decoy himself were a vampire, but that ideal situation probably would never happen.

William, now officially off duty, led the other available team members into their favorite pub. McGreggor's boasted the best selection of beers in town, as well as a good choice of wine. The place didn't belong in the catalog where the upper crust tied one on. The tavern had a wooden floor, where everybody knows your name kind of place. Other than doing their best to go unnoticed, the team blended into the atmosphere just fine.

William settled into a corner booth in the back of the bar. He shoved the table out a few inches since he dwarfed the small bench seat, cramping his team members, Sterling and Sulie, who tried to sit across from him. Raymond, the COLONY leader, joined a moment later, after he had spoken with the waitress and placed all their orders for the evening. Being usuals at the place, the wait staff should have known their orders by heart, but their predatory nature had the vampires blend in. With repeated exposure to a vampire, humans could sometimes remember them, which proved problematic if a vampire wanted to visit his favorite bar for decades without aging. With just one of them speaking to the waitress, there were fewer team members to recall and less chance of the humans becoming aware of them.

Once they were all settled, William had to ask. "How did the administration pick which school to visit today? And why cancel my day off?"

Raymond looked across the table to William. "Because of the safety of the route to the school. Given the preparation time we had, it made it the safest one to select."

"But why call me in on my day off?" William pressed.

There was no hesitation in Raymond's answer. "We were shorthanded and didn't know until the last minute that the President wouldn't be going to the school."

William nodded, allowing the information to sink in. Assuming Jackie was not the only substitute teacher to receive a last minute call, he asked, "What about the substitute teachers called to work at the last minute?"

Raymond sat back in his seat, as if assessing William's questioning. "We dismissed any teacher who had a record, even a childhood misdemeanor, and called in confirmed, background–checked subs." He paused a moment, and then added, "The answer to the question you're dancing around is 'yes'. Every sub was a minority."

William's jaw tightened. "And I was called in because I'm a black man!"

"Not just you," Raymond said. "Ben, as well. Plus, some human agents were called…"

"What the hell!" William said, cutting him off. His nostrils flared and he bared his fangs before realizing the nearby humans now looked his way. Covering his face, he growled deeply.

"Stand down." Raymond scanned the room, noticing the humans had lost interest after a few seconds. "This isn't the first administration that has lied."

The waitress brought a round of beers and a glass of wine to the table and set them down. She smiled and asked about lunch and if everything was all right. The team politely declined the meal and sent her on her way.

Taking a few deep breaths, William said in an even tone, "We shouldn't support his lies. We should stand up for what is right. We need to…"

"No!" Raymond glared at him. "We serve and protect the President. No questions. No judgment."

"It isn't fair," Sulie added, "but we need to look the other way. It's not our place to impose our beliefs on him."

William's body tensed as he eyed the three of them. His eyes stopped at Raymond. "With your pale complexion and teal colored eyes, I wonder if you'd feel the same way if you were on the receiving end of the injustice."

"We are *all* minorities," Raymond said.

Sterling chimed in. "I'm not even accepted within vampire circles because of my human mother."

"And women are only now treated as equals," Sulie added. "We've all faced prejudice in the past."

"I know you're unhappy with the President's actions," Raymond said, taking a deep breath. "And I am sorry not to have told you ahead of time what was happening—but I couldn't risk you making a scene at the school."

William's eyebrow rose in curiosity. He hoped racial stacking was the only agenda the President had, but he had to know for sure. "Does the President have a specific agenda by visiting this school, or by posing with those children?"

William noticed Sulie's eyes slightly widen as though he had touched a raw nerve. She brushed her blonde hair aside and glanced at her brother Raymond.

"Well?" William asked.

"The team is being informed of the circumstances in the morning. But I guess you and Sterling can be told now," Raymond said as he gestured over to Sulie.

Sulie swiveled her head to confirm no one listened in. Then, in that high-pitched voice only the vampires could hear, she said, "The President has had an inappropriate relationship with a member of his staff."

"So?" Sterling asked, using his normal voice. "It's not the first time a president has had an affair. Unless it was a man. *That* would be different."

"It wasn't a man," Raymond said below a whisper,

"however, there is a complication and we can't compel her to forget about the indiscretion."

William's eyes turned cold. The First Lady, a mature woman in her late-forties, had supported her husband through his campaigns, being a single parent while the man traveled, and had gone down the infidelity path with him in the past. She was a quality woman—a woman the President didn't deserve in William's opinion. If he were ever so fortunate to have the love of such a woman, he would treat her like gold.

"Why can't we compel this mistress?" Sterling asked.

Sulie cleared her throat as her eyes scanned the room a second time checking for any eavesdroppers. "She may be pregnant."

"Wait." William stared at Sulie. "You can't tell her condition?"

"Elevated levels of Clomiphene are in her system. It's a fertility drug." Sulie sighed. "A common one usually giving good results for women who *can* get pregnant and want to ensure they do as soon as possible. Her HCG levels, the pregnancy hormone levels, are still low—but gestation may have just started."

"So she is trapping the President." Sterling huffed as he sipped his beer. "Never trust a woman of childbearing years. The man's an idiot."

"Enough," Raymond scolded. "She had a relationship with the President over the last few weeks."

"Who?" William threw his hands up. "I've never seen him with anyone—not that way, at least."

Sterling shook his head. "Yeah, well, that would have been on my watch. I've seen him with someone recently."

"And you didn't stop him from cheating on his wife?"

William would never have allowed such behavior, at least, he would have tried to stop such immoral acts.

Sterling leaned in towards William. "She wasn't a vampire. All I am *required* to do is confirm she is human and that she doesn't intend to harm the President. Unless I touched her," he said, holding up his gloved hands, "I wouldn't have been able to detect the drug in her system. There was no reason to lay a hand on her."

"And since we are unsure if a baby is involved, we don't want to compel her to forget her relationship with the man—at least not until we know for sure," Sulie said.

"We compelled her not to speak to the press." Raymond finished his beer and set the glass down on the table. "The President is aware of the possibility of a pregnancy and has severed ties with the woman, although he does still harbor feelings for her. Right now he is trying to foster a more husbandly and parental appearance in case a leaked announcement comes out in the next few weeks." He took a deep breath. "Honestly, we don't know who else is aware of the relationship, and many times the news is leaked by someone other than the mistress. We understand the First Lady suspects nothing, and the President is doing his best to keep the facts hidden from her and their teenage daughter. Which is why he recently scheduled vacation time for the family at Camp David in a few weeks, and did this trip to visit the kids at the local school," Raymond explained.

It all made sense to William. Something did feel odd about the school trip, and now he understood. He just never would have guessed the real reason. After a moment's pause, he said, "The President doesn't understand how lucky he is, and he's just pissing away the best thing in his life."

Playing with the paper coaster nearest him, William thought about the First Lady. She was a good woman and always supportive. Her charity work alone had always impressed him, although her charities of choice had been more geared towards saving helpless and abused animals. Upon reflection, her recent support of UNICEF and their cause to help children now made sense. She too busied herself painting a domestic, parental picture of her marriage with the President, probably because her husband's staff asked her to without telling her the real reasons why. Most likely, his staff lied and told her he needed to appear more family oriented towards her and their own child.

She would do anything for her husband.

William wished he could find someone half as decent as the First Lady to be his wife. His bed never remained empty for long, but his heart had always been vacant—as well as any cribs and nurseries. His thoughts now focused on his meeting with Ms. Jackie Pearlman from earlier that day. Her body, her passion, her beauty....

William felt self-conscious. His friend Raymond stared at him, and he didn't understand why.

"No," Raymond said directly to him. "Don't put yourself through this again."

God, he couldn't keep anything a secret. Why did his boss always have to pick up on the smallest things. "I don't know what you're talking about...," William said.

"You know," Raymond said. "I can feel your mental patterns as well as hear your thoughts. You're thinking of asking some pretty teacher out."

William tossed the coaster aside. He knew better than to try to cover up his feelings. Raymond could read mental patterns of both humans and vampires by just being near them. If he sat near a vampire, he could even read their thoughts. William bit his lip and tried to think of something to say.

"God. Let's not go through this again." Sterling rolled his eyes. "I suspected your interest in that teacher when you asked me to place her in the handshake spot for the President," Sterling said. "I almost didn't put her there because of that incident a few years ago when I had to help you compel one scared human woman out of the bathroom after you confessed your true nature to her."

William looked away. "That was a long time ago."

"We go through this every year or so," Raymond chided.

Sulie looked from one vamp to the other. "What are you talking about?" She glanced to William and then touched his hand. She took a deep breath, as though now being on the same page. "You're smitten with someone, William."

Sterling shook his head. "They never take the news of you being a vampire well. You always get too emotionally attached to the woman, and another team member has to clean up after you. We always have to compel them to forget your entire relationship."

"Once we get them out of the bathroom or hunt them down after they run from you," Raymond added.

"William," Sulie said, "I hope you do find someone. Don't pay attention to these idiots."

William took a sip of his beer. "The other women of

my past weren't very strong–minded individuals." He pointed at his head. "Not open–minded."

Sterling sipped his beer. "Trust me, it's better just to have your fun and cut them loose. Since the movie <u>Interview with a Vampire</u> came out, you keep thinking women will accept what you are."

William had to think about what Sterling had said for a minute. He guzzled down half his beer as he paused. He didn't even like the movie, but he had been more hopeful over the last few years about a woman's acceptance of him. He doubted the movie had been the cause. Had he not been turned into an immortal vampire, he'd be an old man by now—probably with grandchildren. He didn't want to live a lonely life anymore.

He waved his hands in the air not caring. "I am convinced there is someone for all of us." William realized his current audience may not be the most receptive to his statement, but he didn't care. "We all have that perfect someone who will complete us one day."

Yeah, the words sounded silly coming out of his mouth, but so what? At least Sulie was looking at him and smiling.

Nodding, Raymond added, "I also believe we have a perfect match out there somewhere."

The response surprised William.

"Not me," Sterling said. "You'll never catch me settling down."

That response, however, seemed right on track to William. Sterling, with his GQ pretty–boy looks was a playboy through and through. He glanced from father to son. The two seemed complete opposites of each other. Raymond believed there was only ever one way of doing anything—the moral way. And then there was Sterling. Sex. Drugs. Women—lots of women. Nothing was off the table to him. Sulie, of course, was a hopeful romantic—although he had never seen her date a human or a vampire.

Raymond gave an exasperated look over to his son. "Sterling's opinions aside, I think you have a good chance at finding a woman in your life. Only, find a vampire one. Humans, especially if they don't agree to a turning, can offer too many complications."

"Says the man who never dates," William countered. The affront slipped out, and he immediately wanted to retract the comment. Raymond had been widowed during the birth of his only son. William never knew the complete story, but understood the painful loss Raymond still felt.

"We can try to arrange a marriage through the Vampire Council again," Raymond said, "Maybe this time they'll accept you."

Why was Raymond's answer always going to the Council? The vamp hated that prestigious, self-centered group as much as the other team members. William's turn wasn't sanctioned, therefore they gave him no free blood and no help in the romance department. If he had been gifted a special ability with his turning, the Council might have welcomed him. But no. He had no cool special abilities. He figured they ran in family lines, which was why the three sitting with him all had one.

He took a deep breath. William wasn't sure if he even wanted an arranged marriage, and that is all the Council would offer him.

The server arrived with another round of drinks,

taking away the empty glasses. William noticed Sterling eyeing her bottom as she walked away. Before they left the bar, he bet Sterling would have a date with the woman. His fourth date this week, and today was only Monday.

William wasn't like Sterling. At least, he hoped he wasn't. Sure, as a newly turned vampire, William had dated plenty of women. He wasn't sure what the allure could be, for he certainly still looked the same. Somehow, women were drawn to vampires, which was probably because of a pheromone. Whatever the reason, he sure didn't question the results. At least not in the beginning.

What he wanted now was something better, more intimate... more special. Someone he chose, not a vampire woman selected by the Council.

"Let him be," Sulie chimed in. "I can detect heightened levels of endorphins in his system. If he likes this teacher, so be it."

Raymond took a deep breath and gazed at William. "If this is important to you, try something different."

"What do you mean?" William asked.

"You dated the woman who hid in the bathroom for what? Six months?" When William nodded, Raymond added, "In all that time, you were compelling her, right?"

William's face twisted in disgust. "I don't compel women into my bed."

"Of course you don't," Sulie said, gently touching his hand. "You're a handsome vampire with no need to compel them."

Raymond shook his head. "That's not what I'm talking about. I'm talking about the compulsion to make you appear human to them while you're dating them."

William gave it some thought. "I do compel them to believe that I eat a meal when I take them out to dinner."

"What else?" Sterling asked.

He scratched his head. "I don't know." William paused a moment, but then added, "I compel them to ignore any aging differences they might notice." He stammered a bit. "It's hard to appear the same age to someone for months at a time. Especially when they see you more close up and personal than an average co-worker would."

"And do you bite them?" Raymond pointed down to his neck. "Do you leave any marks or tell tale signs?"

This conversation had become a bit too personal for William's taste. He shifted in his seat, but eventually answered. "I bite them and compel them not to notice, but I seal the puncture marks immediately." He now glanced away. "Sometimes a drop of blood gets on their clothing... or on the sheets, which gets cleaned up as well with compulsion."

"If you want different results, you need to do something different. Do not compel this woman, and do not lie to her." Raymond leaned closer in towards William. "Pursue this human with the truth only. Have her see you as you really are."

A huff came from Sterling's direction. "Too much effort, man."

"But," Sulie interrupted, "this non-compelling plan does have some merit. If William is determined to date a human, let's give him a fresh start and stand behind him."

Raymond nodded. "Or, he could go the easy route and find a female vampire."

William looked at Sulie. "Thank you, Sulie." He then shot a glance at Raymond. "Vampire or not, I was once a human. I don't see anything wrong with dating a human." He took a sip from his beer. "You three were born vampires. There is nothing wrong with human women."

"Except that human women can only give birth to half-breed wimps who aren't really vampires or humans," Sterling said as he glanced at his father.

William glared at Sterling. What the hell? He may have been the only half-breed in the group, and Raymond's only child, but it gave him no right to pick at an old wound his father still nursed.

"Your kid, for the most part, turned out okay." William said to lighten the mood. Raymond had fallen in love and had married a human, so he asked him, "What's your issue with human women?"

Under his breath, Raymond said, "They're weak and die too soon."

CHAPTER 7

*W*illiam walked down the hallway, a small bouquet of wild flowers in his hand. He wasn't scheduled to work at the White House until later in the day, and he thought he might surprise Jackie at her apartment.

He had gotten her address from the school she subbed for by compelling the principal. School policy didn't allow for distributing of personnel information, and since he couldn't compel Jackie not to notice the infraction, he wasn't sure how he would explain how he knew where she lived.

No compelling. No lying. Only the truth. He planned to keep his word, no matter how difficult it would be.

Of course, he could always play the trump card and imply that the Secret Service had other venues for gathering information, which of course they did, and then not give her any details. She would infer that he had gotten the information from them. Not exactly a lie. That would be his plan in case she asked.

Her apartment number was 30B, the last one at the end of the row. As he passed each door, counting up the numbers to thirty, he felt his heart racing. He took a deep breath. There had been plenty of women in his life, but this one felt special.

His mind conjured up an image of Jackie's smile, along with her laugh. She had an angelic presence about her. She stood graceful and confident, even when she reproached him about his job. Something magical existed about Jackie, although he couldn't quite put his finger on what it was.

He tightened his grasp on the flowers and continued making his way towards her door. He had fed this morning, making sure to maintain his current age so she wouldn't notice any changes in his appearance. Also, he didn't want to be quite so hungry while talking with her. Of course, he was always hungry. Her blood smelled like O negative, tasty and delicious.

His blood type matched hers. Maybe not in Rh factor but definitely in type. He wondered if he preferred drinking O negative blood for that reason. The thought never occurred to him before, but the explanation made sense.

A slight smile crossed his lips. Nearly fifty years had passed from his turn, and he still found aspects of vampirism fascinating. Thank goodness Ben had been on the bus with him that day in Alabama. Freedom Riders took a risk of dying for their cause. He was lucky Ben had found him worthy enough to turn when the riot broke out on the bus and he took a fatal blow to the head.

William knocked on Jackie's door, but discovered a second, and then a third knock was needed. All that effort, and she wasn't even home. He turned to leave when a creaking door across the hall caught his attention. William barely caught the woman's glance, but evidently that was enough of an invitation for the neighbor to fully open the door and talk with him.

"I'm looking for Jackie," he said.

The old woman inspected him as though he were a prize package, her eyes settling on the flowers he carried. "Jackie isn't around," she said, smiling. "Are you her new beau?"

Grinning, William asked, "Do you know where she is?"

She glanced down at her watch. After adjusting her glasses, she answered, "It's nearly lunch time. My guess is she's eating lunch."

A vague answer, and virtually no help whatsoever. "All right. Thanks." William nodded and bid his farewell.

She snapped her fingers. "Oh, my memory. She's meeting a Mr. Gary something or other. Gary Appleby? I just can't remember." She shook her head, "Would you like to join me for some tea?"

William felt his chest tighten at the sound of another man's name. "Who's Mr. Appleby?"

"I think he's the manager at Silver Estates. I'm sure she's over there having lunch."

Biting his lip, William knew his fangs had extended slightly. Of course Jackie was being pursued by other suitors. A beautiful woman like her didn't stay available for long.

"Thank you, but I must be going," he said flatly.

"Maybe next time you can stop by for tea," she said as she entered her apartment.

William gave her a polite smile as she closed the

door. He then turned and walked back the way he had come. The woman looked about ninety and possibly lonely. She seemed to be a friendly neighbor—even overly so. Just as he approached the stairs, a flower courier walked past him. William noticed the dozen long stem red roses he carried, and wondered if they were meant for Jackie. He also wondered if they were sent by Mr. Gary Appleby.

William felt a pang of regret and loss as the florist knocked on Jackie's door, only to have the neighbor poke her head into the hallway and strike up a conversation with him. William listened with his vampire hearing as the woman said she'd sign for the flowers, and that they must be from Jackie's gentleman friend Steve. He also overheard her claim she had signed for flowers in the past, and she'd be sure Jackie got them.

She opened the card, intruding upon Jackie's privacy. "From Herman," she announced. "Oh, that's a new one."

Gary? Steve? Herman? Jackie was a sassy and sexy woman, but just how many gentlemen callers did this woman have? He wanted a Mrs. Right, not a woman about town who was a player.

The delivery man made his way down the hallway as William glanced away to avoid eye contact. His eyes now focused on the small cluster of wild flowers he carried. Wilted. Squeezed beyond recognition.

How could he compete with human men who could wine and dine her? It's hard to have a relationship when you have to date around all your meals.

He felt the heaviness of disappointment settle on his heart. He had built Jackie up to be such a perfect find, and now he doubted she was the woman for him. He tossed the wilted flowers into a trash bin on his way out of the apartment building, throwing out his dreams with them.

Jackie led her father to an empty table at Silver Estates. The two set down their trays and put their plates on the table. As they sat, Jackie asked, "What surprise, Daddy?"

He smiled at her. "If they haven't arrived yet, they will. I wanted to send you a little something to brighten your day. They'll probably be delivered by the time you get home tonight."

Jackie wanted to keep prying, but a waitress distracted her by offering a selection of water, lemonade, iced tea or soda.

"Can I bring you anything else?" the waitress asked as she looked at the sweater vest Jackie's father wore.

Jackie looked at her father's sweater. "Daddy, you forgot to wear your nametag." It wasn't exactly policy, but as a courtesy, Silver Estates asked the residents to wear them—not just for the staff, but for the residents who had trouble remembering who people were.

"His name is Herman. I'm his daughter, Jackie."

"Welcome to Silver Estates," the waitress said, smiling at them as she filled their water glasses. "If there is anything you need, please let me know."

Jackie nodded as the woman walked away. It pleased her to have her father living in such a wonderful retirement home. The food looked healthy and plentiful. The menu today was pork chops, fresh apple slices, warm butternut squash soup, a healthy salad, and a variety of desserts.

After she took a bite, she knew the food wasn't as good as her mama's cooking, but pretty darn close. Within minutes, she noticed her father picking at his food. "Daddy, make sure to eat some of your salad. You need greens in your diet."

Herman wrinkled his nose. "The salad dressing has soured."

She picked up the bowl. "Now, don't be like that." She sniffed the food and set the salad back down. "Did you want ranch dressing? Because this is bleu cheese."

He gave her a slight smile as he touched the side of his face. "I left my glasses upstairs."

"Well, if you can't read the signs of what is what, all you got to do is ask. This place has plenty of staff to help you." She halfway stood. "I'll get you a fresh salad."

Holding up his hand, he stopped her. "I'm not all that hungry anyway." He looked past the dining area to the main office. "What did the manager say?"

"He has a crew in your apartment right now fixing your heater. Mr. Appleby seemed very apologetic Daddy. I'm sure he'll have it fixed in no time."

She noticed her father staring near the kitchen door. "Looks like they're bringing out new desserts. Looks like cheesecake."

Jackie felt saddened as her father left the table to fetch them some cheesecake. Cheesecake was her favorite, and her father knew it. The dessert was her mother's favorite, as well. Mama would make her cheesecake from scratch, not with the cream cheese most recipes had these days. She would bake her cake for birthdays, Easter and Christmas—saying the dessert was too rich for everyday food. Her mother always held tight control over their diets when it came to rich, sugary foods, saying it wasn't good to give children a sugar rush, and imply that her father didn't need the excess. Her father remained somewhat slim as an older man, but his cholesterol and heart issues had always been a concern. Jackie decided to ignore the indulgence—at least for now as he settled into his new home. This wonderful retirement home was just minutes from her apartment, and she wanted him to get comfortable and consider it his home as soon as possible.

A heavy emotional weight settled over her. At the time, she felt fortunate to get her father into such a fine place as Silver Estates. With the waiting list, it usually took nearly a year to get in, but a sudden vacancy allowed her to secure her father a spot after only two weeks. Now, with the loss of her job, she worried if she'd be able to afford the place. Her father paid for most of the cost, but she had fudged the numbers to him so he wouldn't suspect she financially helped him. She had researched retirement homes in the area. They were either all too expensive, too far away, or just terribly unpleasant places where she didn't want her father to live out the rest of his life. Paying a little extra a month herself to secure something this nice was worth the personal cost. She only hoped she could still afford the place now.

He came back to the table and set two wedges of cheesecake down. He frowned as he took his seat. "What's wrong, sweetie?"

She waved her hand dismissively. "Nothin' you need to worry about."

His eyebrows furrowed as he took a good look at her. "Is everything with your job all right?"

Biting her lip, she gave him a wry smile. "Yes, Daddy. It's all good."

He scratched his head and still studied her. "Is a man troubling you? Because if a man has broken your heart again..."

Jackie sighed, which caused him to pause mid–sentence.

"It *is* a man," he accused.

She smiled back at her father. She hadn't been on a date in months. She hadn't... *been* with a man for even longer. This wasn't a conversation she wanted to share with him.

"Your mama always said baking was a way to share your soul with those you love." He scooted one plate of cheesecake closer to her. "It's not your mama's, but it looks good."

She glanced at the cake. It was nice to hear him quote her mother, who always had nice sayings about life. Jackie cleared her throat and mentally chided herself. She didn't want to fall apart in front of her father. She missed her mother terribly, but wanted to be strong for him.

So she thought about something else she wanted to share with her father. She doubted he had been watching the news lately since he seemed so busy with his move. In fact, she had wanted to tell him about the meeting with the President since the moment they had sat down at the table. She filled him in on the presidential things only, omitting she was subbing at the school and any ideas she may have had about the minority numbers being odd to her. What she didn't skip was the part of how the gorgeous agent had selected her out of everyone to shake the President's hand. She had been so surprised after he admitted to having selected her, but she didn't have enough time to ask him about it since he had to leave and tend to the President.

Her father had smiled through the entire tale. "You must have caught his eye for him to give you such an honor as shaking the President's hand."

"Maybe so." She didn't go into detail, but did mention the agent was extremely handsome. She couldn't stop thinking about him.

Herman beamed a smile back to her. "And he has a good, solid job working for the President."

"An agent who allows racial inequality in his job, but I guess it's still a solid job." She regretted making the snide comment, and wished she had censored herself the second the sentence left her mouth.

Her father cleared his throat. "Now, don't be like that." When she stared into his eyes, she saw a stern look about him. "Do you remember a show you liked as a kid that was called Star Trek?"

Remember it? She loved the show as a kid. Of course, she liked the original series the best. "Lt. Uhura was always my favorite."

"I know," Herman said.

Jackie stared at her father. There were days he couldn't remember what he had for lunch the day before, and there were times he could remember the most minute details. It was nice to have him fully here and in the moment. "What about the show?"

"Your mother didn't like all the space stuff, but she and I both agreed it was a good show for you to watch. Do you want to know why?" When Jackie shook her head, Herman continued, "Because of the actress Nichelle

Nichols who played Lt. Uhura. Back in the 1960s when she started in the show, her small and somewhat degrading part upset her. She almost quit until she met Dr. Martin Luther King Jr., who told her she needed to be on the show. You see, that television show was based in the future, and he believed that a black face needed to be on the bridge to encourage the next generation of Americans to believe in equality."

Jackie always enjoyed the show and had never heard the story before. Lt. Uhura was always a hero of sorts to her, and she now realized the load the actress must have had to endure to remain on film back in the days with segregation and other racial inequalities. Jackie looked at her father. "How do you know all this?"

"She did an interview way back in the day. Anyway, if this young man of yours is holding down a job that only a few decades ago wouldn't have been open to him, then he's paving the way for the next generation and the one after that. He's doing more for equality than you can even imagine just by being in his position."

Jackie smiled at the revelation. Her father had a good point. Even a few decades ago, she wouldn't have been allowed to teach at her school since white children attended. Her purse hung from the chair and she retrieved the agent's business card from it. "He did give me his card," she said as she handed it proudly to her father.

His hand danced over the card as he turned it over. He gave the card back to her, but not before he could let out a disappointed sigh.

Jackie palmed the card. "What's wrong?"

"I thought it'd be neat to see the presidential seal or Secret Service stamp."

Jackie studied the plain white card and a frown crossed her face as she realized her father was right. This wasn't an official government card with the Secret Service or FBI emblem on it. This was the man's personal business card having only his name and phone number. She had seen plenty of cards like this in the past, and they were always given out by men who only wanted one thing from a woman.

Good Lord. He had played her.

When he had given her the card, she had hoped he might be able to help her with her petition for the school funding—and maybe a whole lot more on a personal level. Now, looking at the man's information, she read between the lines. He was a user of women. He had this card at the ready to give to any cute woman he came across, and probably handed out several a day. She tossed the card into her purse and then picked up her fork, diving into the cheesecake. She'd be damned if she were going to be William Wardell's next conquest.

CHAPTER 8

*J*ackie sat nervously on the brown overstuffed chair in the corner of Starbucks. She knew the place well since it was so near to her old school, even with her strict discipline of only enjoying one purchased coffee a week. She waited for Principal Bob Monroe to show up.

Why did the man want to meet with her? And why now? The last time she had seen the man, he had laid her off. The fault of her job loss didn't rest on Bob's shoulders, but she did, sort–of, want to shoot the messenger. Taking a deep breath and blowing through the small slit in the lid of her coffee cup, she focused her attention on her hot cup of coffee.

She didn't have to wait long. Bob entered the shop, waved to her, and then ordered himself a hot beverage. Once he had his coffee in hand, he took a seat next to her.

As she waited for him to talk, it occurred to her that perhaps her petition had caused trouble for the school, or had threatened Bob's job. She certainly hoped Bob was strong enough to stand his ground and demand the changes that were desperately needed. Bob was a good family man with four kids, and she hoped his position wasn't in jeopardy; he needed his job.

Well, she needed a job, too. She sighed slightly. Whatever he needed to tell her must be important since he had asked for her to meet with him right away. It wasn't as though she was busy. Other than the subbing job from last week, she had nothing financial lined up on the horizon. She didn't even want to get her hopes up that he brought her here for good news.

Bob placed his coffee cup on the small table as he sat across from her. "I'm so glad you could meet with me, Jackie," he said, smiling. "How have you been?"

His smile defused her worry, and for a moment it felt like old times. She shared with him her recent trip to California, the breakup with Steve, and her father's move into a nursing home. Overall, having an old friend to talk with felt nice.

"My goodness," she chuckled. "Just listen to me talk. I haven't even asked about your wife and kids."

"She's fine," he replied. "The kids are the same. School work, track, and basketball. Our lives are filled with car pools."

"You know what they say. It takes a village to raise a kid."

"That's right." Bob sat straighter in his seat and cleared his throat. "An anonymous donation has been made to the school," he announced. "Which is why I asked for you to meet with me."

Jackie sipped her coffee and then set the hot cup down on the table. "A monetary donation, I'm guessing."

"Yes. And, before you ask, I don't know who the bene-factor is, just that a sizable amount was donated."

Her jaw tightened as she eyed him. "I do love a good mystery. Go on."

"The funding is already in place. There are some stipu-lations for tapping into the funds, though. One is that we bring back one of our cut programs, the other is that we bring you back as a teacher within that program."

"Me?" she stammered. "Why would this benefactor want me?"

Bob shook his head. "No explanation was given."

No explanation? Damn, that meant the donator prob-ably knew her. Who could it be? Was it her ex-boyfriend Steve? As a pension fund baby, he had some dispensable money. She didn't like the idea of being in debt to the sleaze, but it was a job—of sorts. A job worth looking into. "What program would be brought back?"

"Music and Art."

Music, chorus, and anything liberal arts related had been cut across the school district. Her face whitened. She couldn't draw a straight line or carry a tune, and had no clue how to play a musical instrument, but she needed a job. "What would I be expected to do?" she asked, sitting on the edge of her seat.

He sank into his chair. "Now, Jackie. I can hire you, but the board needs to approve the district reinstating you as a teacher. I don't expect there to be a problem; I think they'll take you back right away. I just want to make sure you would be interested in the offer."

She took a deep breath, not realizing she had been holding it in. She couldn't have expected her good fortune. "Is this full-time?"

"Since the funds are in place, we can bring you on–board as a temporary music teacher full–time, and in the Fall, after Ms. Winters retires, we can slide you into her spot for teaching fifth graders. You'll already be on staff and not considered a new hire at that point in time, so the transition will be simple." He paused and looked at her. "That is, if a third grade position isn't also available then."

Jackie would prefer to remain a third grade teacher, but had taught fifth grade in the past—although, many years ago. She wouldn't be the lead teacher for that group of children, so she'd have to rely upon the fifth grade teachers to share their curriculum with her. She had known of Ms. Winters' retirement plans, so it seemed like a good solution to her current money issues.

The unanswered question still nagged at her. Who did she have to thank for her good fortune?

CHAPTER 9

William had gone out to a nightclub with Sterling, but the time was late, and he wanted to leave. He hadn't been out with his COLONY buddy in quite some time and regretted tonight's outing almost immediately. Plenty of women had been drawn to them and their vampire charm, like moths to a flame. Sterling seemed quite pleased with the choices for the evening, but William felt underwhelmed. None were of the caliber of Jackie, and the evening served more of a reminder of how much he wanted to go out with her than it was a distraction to forget her.

He often found himself thinking of her, especially since he donated so much money to the school district. All the kids in the area needed a music program, and William felt he only fixed the problem with a tiny band-aid since only one school benefited from his donation. Sarpy Elementary, where Jackie had taught, had over 600 kids. It was only one school of many within the inner city, but one of the poorest. He should have felt pride in his efforts, but only wished he could do more.

He also felt anxious. Jackie accepted the job over two months ago, and from what he could tell, she was a good fit. Even though he wanted to see her again, he kept his visits to the school low profile so he wouldn't bump into her. He didn't want her to suspect he was the anonymous donor, but after having visited the school once, he knew he had to volunteer as a big brother to some of the young teens who desperately needed a father figure—even if it was just to play basketball with them after school or to hang out with them on his days off.

Although he knew he shouldn't pursue Jackie, he had promised himself he wouldn't lie to her. At this point, his actions seemed more of an exercise to see if the tactics would work on a woman, and he ran through scenario after scenario in his mind as to what he would say to her if he bumped into her.

Finding himself on autopilot, he left Sterling and drove into the city to a small apartment he kept. He spent most of his time there instead of driving to the remote suburbs where the members of the COLONY shared a mansion, that they affectionately called Fang Manor.

Spacious Fang Manor allowed him to feel at ease, but the government-supplied home came with restrictions. No visitors allowed. Period. The place offered some nice amenities, such as maid service, and since it was listed as a private military hospital, it also came with weekly blood deliveries. The place seemed perfect for raising a family, but none of the COLONY members, except Raymond, had a family—and even Raymond's son was fully grown.

William sighed. Jackie seemed more of a city girl. She may not even like living in a big mansion in the middle of nowhere. She was probably a party–goer with her dance card filled each night. He swallowed the lump in his throat as he gathered his mail and then walked up the flight of stairs to enter his lonely apartment. Once in, he tossed his keys onto a nearby table and looked through his mail.

A large green envelope caught his attention. The return address was from the school district, so he opened the letter immediately. Scanning through the letter, he realized it was an invite to an annual private auction held by the school. It was a masquerade party and fund–raiser with all teachers, administrative staff, and board members invited. He had seen information about the event while visiting the school periodically over the last few weeks, but hadn't realized he would also be invited.

His interest in the event was low, until he read the fine print. The proceeds of the auction directly benefited the school district, but more specifically, the hosting school received an additional twenty percent of all the funds collected. Scanning the invite, he saw that this year's event was to be held at Sarpy Elementary School – the school where Jackie taught.

He stared at the invite wondering if Jackie would attend. As a fund–raiser, he figured there was a good chance she might, especially since her own school bene-fited so greatly.

Now he didn't know what to do.

He definitely wanted to see Jackie again, but wasn't sure how he could fake not eating at the party. He felt his chest tighten so he took a deep breath. What if she brought a date with her? God, what if she didn't? He couldn't lie to her if he wanted to pursue her, but deep down he remained afraid of her running away from him screaming in terror once he revealed to her what he truly was.

He decided to stop torturing himself with the what–ifs of life, and to shower and get dressed. His duty tonight at the White House started soon, and he didn't have the time to waste.

During his shave, he stared at his hazy reflection in the mirror. Damn. His age was off. He looked a good six or seven years older than when Jackie had met him. A few more gray hairs had developed, as well as a couple of wrinkles around his eyes. He had to fix that if he bumped into her at the party.

Walking to the refrigerator, he powered on a small water bath. It was used for warming baby bottles, but it also warmed blood to the perfect degree. He opened the refrigerator and pulled out the bag of blood. Other than the blood, and some bottles of wine, nothing else was in the refrigerator.

From the utensil drawer, he got out two syringes. He filled them with blood and dipped them into a warm water bath. The amount of blood would be just enough to give him back those missing years. With his dinner warming, he waited until the machine beeped.

As a recently turned vamp, he rarely had to hunt for food since bagged blood had always been around for his convenience. He had bitten his girlfriends over the years, but a lover's nip wasn't the same as a full feeding. He took a deep breath as he felt his fangs extend. He would inject the blood directly into his bloodstream, bypassing the need for his spleen to convert the dinner from the digestive tract into his circulatory one. Still, his fangs popped out on queue with every meal.

His eyes blackened and he swallowed the saliva pooling in his mouth in anticipation of his next meal.

Buzzzzz

Finally! Grabbing the syringe, he plunged the needle into his arm. He gasped at the wonderful sensation as the new human blood mingled with the older blood in his veins. Vampires couldn't produce their own blood; they had to live on borrowed blood. As the blood circulated and aged within a vampire's body, it slowly thickened and turned purple—aging the vampire in the process. Over time, the blood within the vampire's veins would become a blackened goo. The cells of the body aged until new blood was supplied, or until the blood could no longer be used, and the vampire aged to the point where his body turned to dust.

William dispensed the second syringe into his arm, allowing the dose of crimson delight to travel the same path as the first. The wrinkles around his eyes ironed themselves out, his skin became more elastic, and he knew any aged spots had already disappeared, as well as any gray hair. Yes, five plus years could make a difference in a person's appearance.

He closed his eyes as he reclined on his couch. Tingling sensations spread across his body until the onset of bloodlust hit him. His body had replenished itself, and now he had an innate desire to mate. That's when his mind focused on the party and the possibility of seeing Jackie again.

CHAPTER 10

*J*ackie arrived at her apartment later than she expected. Spending the last few hours at the art supply store was not her idea of fun, but the task was necessary. She tossed the mail and her newly purchased art and music supplies onto her kitchen table and then walked to the TV and turned the set on. The late evening news blared.

Great. The time was even later than she had thought.

She couldn't remember the last time she relaxed in a hot tub and sipped a glass of wine while listening to soft jazz, or the last time she read a book just for the mere pleasure of reading a book. Even the last movie she went to was that stupid vampire movie, which was quite a while ago now.

A green envelope on the table caught her attention, so she picked the letter up—hoping it wasn't what she dreaded it to be. Unfortunately, the invite proved to be exactly what she had feared. There had been memos circulating around the school, as well as follow-up emails about the event, so she wasn't too surprised to receive the formal notification by mail.

She stared at her invitation to the annual masquerade party she now held in her hand. How did the summer get here so fast? Between the visits with her father, which were nice, but taking up a couple of nights a week, and the new art supplies and techniques she was learning, the time just flew by.

Knowing she would attend, like she did every year, she wrote the date on her wall calendar in the kitchen. No other special events, specifically any dates, were marked for the month, so she figured she had at least one social event to look forward to. Her own school would be hosting, so she would definitely be there.

She set the invite down on the kitchen counter next to some freshly washed paint brushes, and then walked to the refrigerator. Opening the door to the freezer, she searched the selection of frozen foods until she found the frozen cheesecake. She gave a wry smile as she took the cake out and set the frozen pastry on the counter. "Not for dinner," she said to herself. The small cake would make a nice, yet a bit oversized, dessert. Finding the frozen, low-fat, single-sized lasagna dinner, she placed the meal in the microwave and waited the three minutes for her "Gourmet Italian Dinner" to be ready.

Her kitchen table was filled with art supplies and one of the chairs held a box of music recorders. Jackie took in a deep breath and let the air out slowly. She wasn't cut out to be a music and arts teacher, and she felt as though she was letting the kids down. There had been no complaints, and several of the children seemed to genuinely enjoy the classes she taught, but she wished she was either better suited for the task or for the summer to end so she'd be put into the freed–up fifth grade position.

After chopping up a small salad, she placed her meal on the table with a glass of water and sat down. The more veggies she could add to the meal the better she thought, especially since she still eyed the cheesecake on the counter.

She didn't even get into her second bite of food before her cell phone rang. The familiar tune from Gloria Gaynor "I Will Survive" sounded, so she knew it was Steve. Damn it. Of course he wanted to talk with her, but she wasn't about to pick up the phone. That football coach had obviously received his invite to the party. Last year they went in matching costumes and had even won the auction for a date–night dinner at an elite restaurant in town.

The song stopped playing, and now a text came in.

She stared at the phone, not even tempted to answer it. He could leave her messages, and maybe she'd read and listen to them later.

She pushed the salad aside and reached for the cheese-cake and dove in. Steve was just a loser, not worthy of her time. But, she did enjoy having someone to talk to, to touch, and to be held by. She nearly finished the cake when something on the TV caught her eye. The broadcast was a presidential briefing at the White House.

She turned up the volume and realized that it wasn't a huge news conference, like the state of the union address, but a small press release. Standing near the podium was the agent she had met a few months ago, William. She sighed heavily as she took in the sight of him. Clean shaven, expensive suit cut to fit him perfectly, and she bet he was packing a weapon. Yeah, she thought that to be incredibly sexy.

She bit her lip as she thought what else he might be *packing* under that suit. She had thought of him often over the last few months, and not necessarily in a choir–girl sort of way. The camera scanned with a closeup and his doe–soft brown eyes were highlighted on her TV set. Her breath caught when she saw them up close. He appeared sensitive and secure, yet strong and forceful.

That man was just the whole package. She licked her lips. How soft were William's lips? How passionately did he kiss?

Next, the President was announced and he walked up to the podium. He wore a sweater instead of a suit jacket, the kind of sweater her father and Mr. Rogers from the old children's show always wore. It gave the man a fatherly image as he began speaking. She listened as he gave a short speech about family values and living the American dream. He then denounced the allegations that he was having an affair with an intern—claiming to love his wife too much to put her through such stress. The details of the affair indicated it happened several months ago, and that the intern was dismissed from the White House due to the rumors she may have been pregnant.

Jackie's eyes rolled. Even the President couldn't keep it in his pants! Why were all men after just one thing, and one thing only? And once they got what they wanted, they looked for something different? Jackie never thought she'd have something in common with the First Lady, but here it was.

A short video of a very slender twenty–something year old intern refusing to talk with the press aired on the television. Jackie studied the young, slim woman. She was either a home-wrecker or a naive girl believing the President would toss everything aside just for her. A book deal would probably come soon enough. Her thin waist indicated to Jackie that the woman wasn't pregnant, so soon the intern's fifteen minutes of fame would most likely end.

Jackie scowled as the President ended the announcement and left the press room. She always liked the First Lady, and, even though she didn't like the budget cuts her husband's administration was doing, Jackie hoped the woman would find happiness in whatever she decided to do.

A tear rolled down Jackie's cheek and a heaviness settled upon her heart. Why did love have to be so complicated? It was supposed to be that you meet the love of your life and grow old with them. Someone to always be there for you. Someone in sickness and in health. Someone... someone to hold you in their arms as you lay dying.

She set down her fork and pushed the cheesecake aside. Why did everything always remind her of her mother? She reached for a tissue on the table and blew her nose. Her mother wasn't very old when she died, but she also wasn't that young either. She had lived a good life, with a good man. She had made that leap for love and, even though Jackie suspected their marriage had ups and downs, her mother always had someone to be with her. Someone to love her.

Gloria Gaynor's tune sounded once again on her phone. Against her better judgement, Jackie answered.

CHAPTER 11

*W*illiam was desperate. He couldn't go to the party alone, so he called in a favor to the only female vampire friend he had.

"You want me to be your date?" Sulie shook her head as she walked with William down the Hall of Columns in the Capitol building. "A masquerade party?"

"I have a plus-one," William said. Overall, bringing a date made sense, but now he was second guessing his decision. As a good friend, Sulie owed him a favor or two, but she always meddled into other people's businesses. Opening the door and letting her into his personal life felt like playing with fire, and it was a sign of how low he had sank in his love life. He hated it.

Sulie slowed her pace as they arrived at the connecting hallway that would lead her to her next meeting. "So let me get this straight," she began. "The school district invited you to their annual costume ball…"

"Masquerade auction. I don't think there will be any dancing."

"Uh, huh." Sulie's mouth twisted as she stared at William, which made him feel uneasy. "The school district where that pretty teacher worked at just happened to send you an invite?"

William bit his lip as the two of them paused in the hallway. "I didn't say it was her district."

"Puh-lease." Sulie rolled her eyes. "You've been depressed ever since you met her and decided not to date her."

He would have protested, but he knew his mood as of late had been somewhat surly.

Sulie shook her head. "Invite *her* to go with you, not me."

He thought about the parade of men Jackie had in her life. He didn't need the rejection. "Not an option." He cleared his throat. "Look, if you don't want to be my plus-one you don't have to. I would prefer not to show up alone though."

"Which is why you should ask this teacher out." Sulie looked at her watch, and William knew he was holding her up.

"She has a boyfriend," William blurted out. "I'm sure she received an invite, as well, and I just don't want to show up stag."

Sulie's look softened. "How do you *know* she's seeing someone? Did she tell you?"

William rubbed the back of his neck. He was also running late to his next meeting, but wanted to secure a date for the blasted party. "Not exactly. Her neighbor hinted there was a man in her life." He took in a deep breath. "Several men actually. I doubt I'd stack up against all of them, especially if I can't even take her out to a meal without lying to her."

Sulie grinned from ear-to-ear. "You're pathetic." She slowly walked down the hallway to her meeting, but then turned round with a devilish grin on her face. "I'll pick out the costumes."

He didn't trust her smile. "I think we just need masks," he protested.

"You'll wear what I pick out and give no complaints."

CHAPTER 12

*J*ackie felt ridiculous as she arrived at the school district's annual costume party. It wasn't her costume that fueled her mood, since she knew she looked hotter than hell in it, but something else.

Shimmering gold silk draped from her shoulders and cascaded down her back, leading to a full–length skirt which nearly trailed the floor. Her brightly colored mask was an arrangement of feathers and beads that flattered her face and hair. The costume gave her figure an hour-glass appearance, showing off her recent, and now frequent, workouts at the gym.

No. She wasn't regretting her outfit. What made her feel silly was her companion for the evening. At first she thought dressing as the Phoenix, with its rebirth from ashes to a living creature, would suit her present circum-stance—namely leaving a dead–end relationship and finally deciding to go out and, perhaps, find the love of her life. Instead, she entered the school's gym accompanied by her ex–boyfriend Steve.

She should have dressed as a doormat.

She hadn't exactly planned the date, but his call last week caught her off guard. If she hadn't been feeling sad, she might have let him leave a voicemail message again. But, no. She had to answer the damn phone. Immediately, his smooth talking ways, with sweet remembrances of good times in the past, began chipping away at her better judgment.

She was hopeless.

To make matters worse, Steve arrived late to pick her up and dressed in the same costume as last year—a vampire. The black cape and form–fitting dark clothing looked good on the man. After all, he was a gym teacher with muscles to spare. The mask he wore was just basic white. No frills, no decorations… just bone chilling white.

To finish the ensemble, Steve bought a pair of the cheap plastic fangs you'd normally find in every costume store around Halloween. The man looked strikingly good and nerdy at the same time. It was an odd combination, but at least he wouldn't try to kiss her while wearing the cheap fangs. Well, he better not.

At no point in time would anything physical occur between them, and Steve was definitely not going to stay the night with her. Never again. Catching him cheating on her with the French teacher was too much to bear, especially since she felt as though she had been the laughing stock of the entire school. Her 'wash day' granny panties and unshaven legs would guarantee no hanky-panky tonight.

And what about Steve's rep at the school after the

breakup? He paraded around like a peacock, while the skank he dallied with left the school humiliated. And good riddance to her.

Throughout it all, Jackie held her head up high and pretended the break-up didn't bother her. In truth, she knew deep down Steve wasn't the one. Having someone to come home to was always nice, and recently she realized that she had indeed been lonely—if not a little depressed.

Why couldn't she have what her parents had? They had a relationship that survived for decades, filled with love. Surely she wasn't asking too much out of life to have someone who would treat her with respect.

As she crossed the gym floor, she felt every eye on her, and she assumed she knew everyone's thoughts. Once a cheater, always a cheater. She wasn't a fool, but she knew some people, women included, did fall off the fidelity wagon at some point in time. Not that she would ever do such a thing. If a remorseful cheater attended a couple's therapist, she suspected that a relationship may survive. But that wouldn't be her and Steve's story. There was nothing there to save.

As a pension-fund baby, Jackie suspected Steve was the benefactor of the money donated to the school, but that didn't mean she owed him anything for his deed. He played coy and pretended not to understand what she was talking about the few times she mentioned the donation to him—which was why she avoided him at the school, never venturing towards the gym. By not acknowledging what he had done, he didn't even allow her to graciously give a curt thank you and move on. And that drove Jackie crazy.

With the whispers now forming around her from her co-workers, she decided to ditch her date and seek out the bar.

~

William entered the school with Sulie, his black cape flowing behind him. The idea of coming to the party as a vampire was a grotesque pun on reality, but Sulie would hear none of his protests—not even about the silly all-white mask.

On the other hand, Sulie was dressed as a she-devil. A *sexy* she-devil. Red leather pants cut below the navel, a tail trailing out the back, and a low-cut red-sequin tank top which allowed "the girls" to nearly pop right out. Her outfit was ridiculous, and he was tempted to put a few single bills into her pants to let her know what he thought of the costume, but he didn't want to be on Sulie's bad side. Not with her temper.

"This school is a mess," Sulie said, commenting on the paint-chipped walls and graffiti along the hallway leading to the gym. "I can see why they need a fundraiser."

"All of this," he said, pointing around, "is cosmetic. What they really need are better textbooks and computers."

Sulie nodded in agreement. "Let's hope this event is successful then. Based on how packed the parking lot was, I'm assuming every staff member in the district is here."

William walked with Sulie into the gym and followed her to a corner of the room. "This place is crowded. Do you know if your dream woman is here?" she asked.

William studied the room, but with so many people

standing about, he wasn't sure if he could find her. "I'm not sure. With everyone wearing a mask tonight, I think it'll be difficult to even spot her."

"But she is coming?" Sulie asked.

"I'm guessing she received an invite, but that's no guarantee she'll be here." William scanned the room once more. Why did every party at a school gym look the same? Crepe paper, balloons, tables of baked goods and soda were about. As much as he'd like to think he was at a mature masquerade party, this looked just like every high school dance he ever attended—except he had gone to an all Negro school back in the day.

"There's a table," Sulie pointed to the far corner of the gym. "The silent auction requires signatures. If she's bid on anything, we'll see her name on those record logs."

William led Sulie over to the auctions. The table was filled with onlookers, and he noticed the teachers of the school took their bidding very seriously. The auction held romantic dinner giveaways, bed & breakfast stays, bottles of wine, and everything else you would expect for a silent auction. Every item had at least five bids. The prices began somewhat low, but then again, these were teacher salaries. The teachers' dedication to this event impressed him.

Sulie gave a slight whistle. "This deal is pretty good." She looked at William. "A carriage ride around town followed by dinner for two at a very exclusive country club." She picked up the pen and handed it to William. "You should bid on this."

Glancing at the bids, William considered the auction. An 'exclusive country club' back in the day would mean no Negroes or Jews allowed, now the term meant filthy rich. Times, they were a changin'.

If Jackie were to lose all her suitors and take an interest in him, he would love to take her to such a place. He noticed the largest bid came from a guy named Steve. Regardless, William signed his name and pushed the auction bid by nearly twice the amount already offered.

CHAPTER 13

*A*fter ditching her date and getting a drink at the bar, Jackie approached the principal, Bob Monroe, at the refreshment stand. The man was dressed as Superman, but his thinning hair and partial toupee gave away his secret identity. The man's wife was somewhere around, probably dressed as Lois Lane and flitting from table to table to talk with everyone. The poor woman rarely got to go anywhere with the two of them working full-time jobs and the kids at home. Her mingling left Bob open game for Jackie to corner.

"So, Bob," she said as she lifted her mask just enough for him to recognize her. "I know you don't want to tell me who the man was that donated to the music and arts program…"

Bob held up his hand as he laughed. "For the thousandth time, I'm not going to tell you."

From the sound of his slurred speech, Jackie knew Bob was enjoying his time off from the kids, and had probably already downed a few beers and maybe a scotch. It was the perfect time to pump him for information.

She smiled coyly at him. "Well, I already know who donated the money."

"You do?" Bob grabbed a sugar cookie, managing to say, "Good for you," just before shoving the tasty treat into his mouth.

"I won't tell anyone the secret."

Bob eyed her suspiciously and then pointed at her. "You don't know."

Jackie confidently stared him in the eyes. "Oh, I know." She leaned in closer. "And I know he's here tonight."

Bob looked around, carefully scrutinizing the crowd. She suspected the masks and alcohol made it hard to judge, but Bob knew whom to look for. She noticed his eyes stop on the man with the vampire costume standing at the auction table.

Damn. She had been right.

"It's Mr. Dracula," she said.

"Shhhh," Bob managed to slur out. "It's a secret."

She glared at the vampire and she-devil vixen. Not that she cared, but how dare they stand that close together and be that affectionate as they read through the bid items! Steve was at this party with her, not that devil. Was it too much to ask that he not try to pick up another woman while already on a date?

The devil smiled and patted him on the arm, as though she were to be the recipient of the auction if Steve won. Jackie's eyes narrowed in on Steve. It really wasn't her place to be jealous, especially since she had no loving feelings towards the man. But the betrayal of what he was doing, and especially since it was again on school prop-erty, made Jackie madder than hell.

Once again, he'd made a fool of her in front of her coworkers, and this time she had set herself up by agreeing to be the man's date. Noticing mini cheesecakes sitting on the refreshment stand, Jackie bid good–bye to her diet and reached for the creamy pastry.

CHAPTER 14

The clock was ticking, and William knew he only had a few minutes left of Sulie's help to find Jackie. He pulled out his mobile phone from his heavily weighted cape pocket, and noticed no new calls had come in from the team. The schedule had Sulie working the ten o'clock shift, and she would be leaving soon. He wasn't working tonight, but was on call, so he thought he might leave with Sulie—even before the announcement of the raffle winners.

He again walked the perimeter of the party, passing tables filled with district coworkers who were either tipsy, bored, or gossiping amongst themselves. Sulie had seen Jackie once on television when she shook hands with the President, so she went to check the two closest ladies' rooms. William suspected Jackie had only made an appearance and had left the party within minutes of arriving, but he appreciated Sulie checking none–the–less.

With William's vampire hearing, he heard someone mention Jackie's name, so he sought out a table of ladies sitting quietly in the corner of the room gossiping about many of the party-goers. The gaggle of hens clucked about everyone's costumes, their hairstyles, and how drunk some of their coworkers were getting.

Could these ladies here themselves talking? How much cattier could they even be?

William understood any social gathering lent itself to an onslaught of nosy busybodies who had nothing better to do than to put others down, he just had never experienced it before. He was spying and getting the information he so desperately wanted, though—so wasn't going to complain.

He stood against the wall behind their table, blending in the best he could, and listening. The phrase "a fly on the wall" crossed his mind, and he felt silly for such a guise, but if it helped him track Jackie down, so be it.

He thought to compel them to continue talking about Jackie, but these ladies seemed more than willing to focus on her and her date. The women didn't even notice William hiding in the shadows as they viciously tore into their coworker.

The ladies ranted about Jackie's insane decision to give Steve another chance, and how desperate she must be to take the cheating bastard back. They also criticized her outfit. They thought the gold dress made her resemble the Academy Awards Oscar statue, and that the feathered mask made her look like an ostrich who had just pulled her head from the sand.

Of the four ladies, only one offered a kind word for Jackie. It was a backhanded compliment though, as William assumed she tried to fit in with the rest of the spiteful women. The somewhat-kind woman mentioned

Jackie's father and how difficult it must be to mourn the loss of her mother and settle her father into a retirement home.

While listening, he gathered Jackie was struggling, and nearly failing, as a teacher of art and music. Through the three ladies' loathing remarks, William could tell the fourth lady was trying to defend Jackie. She offered excuses of time spent with her father and with students, giving them tutoring and support in all their other subjects. William realized that Jackie spent nearly every moment of her day either at the school, with the students, or with her elderly father.

It wasn't until one of the snide women distastefully commented on Jackie's lack of a husband, citing her lack of a dating life over the last few months, that William realized he had misjudged Jackie's love life. She wasn't a player. Steve had played her. What cut William deeply was the fourth woman's comment that she thought Jackie still loved Steve. The remark was met with a barrage of not–so–polite comments by the other women at the table.

William had heard enough. He needed to find a woman trimmed in gold and... tell her what? That she needed better friends? Yes. That she deserved a better man in her life than Steve? Probably. Tell her that he, a vampire, was the man of her dreams? Not quite so much.

He needed to find Sulie and get a woman's opinion, but not until he compelled the four ladies to no longer speak ill of Jackie.

CHAPTER 15

"*T*here you are!" Sulie said as she pulled on William's arm, stopping him mid–stride as he crossed the room in search of Jackie. "You won't believe what I just went through."

Hearing the half–disgust, but also some humor in her voice, William led Sulie to a side table out of earshot of other party goers. "Did you find her?"

"What? No. I didn't see Jackie anywhere. But I witnessed a steamy scene in the second bathroom," she said, smiling. "A heated scene between a man and a very drunk woman."

William shrugged as he glanced around the room at the drunk people. "I would never have guessed teachers and guidance counselors would party this hard."

"This is an end–of–year, possibly end–of–career, event for these people. I suspect they project a serious image during work hours. Anyway," Sulie said, giving William a wry smile. "I thought I walked in on you and Jackie having sex in one of the stalls."

"Me?"

"I heard them at first, then the man walked out of the stall with his black cape waving proudly behind him." She tugged at William's cape. "He even wore a white mask like yours. I thought he was you until I smelled the human blood coursing in his veins, and the stench of food on his breath."

"Seriously? *That* is what told you it wasn't me? Not that I wouldn't jump on a drunk woman in a filthy public restroom?"

"Well, there is that," Sulie said. "But for a split second I thought *he* was *you*. The man also winked at me—and not in a friendly way. He then hit on me, even while his last conquest dressed herself only a few feet away."

William knew his friend all too well. "What did you do to him?"

"What?" she said coyly. "Little ol' me?"

William's eyebrow rose questioningly.

"Right now he's cleaning the bathrooms on this floor. Once he's done, he'll clean the ones on the second floor, and then go home and get some rest. Starting tomorrow, he's volunteering at a woman's shelter one day a month for a year."

Rolling his eyes, William said, "He got off easy."

"I was in a relatively good mood. After all, he did find me attractive. And I suppose, in a way, his desire for me was a compliment."

Overall, the man's behavior did not shock William. Plenty of players existed in the world, but the man's flagrant bravado of the situation seemed brazen. William could guess the explanation. "Maybe he was drunk."

When Sulie gave him a hurt look, William ran the

remark through his mind again. "I didn't mean he'd have to be drunk to hit on you. But to engage in sexual activity with all your coworkers and the board members only a few feet away, well... the idea makes no sense."

"I don't know," Sulie said. "If the timing is right and the passion is hot... a tryst in a secluded spot, maybe even behind locked doors, would be acceptable."

William's mouth fell open. "Is there a story behind that, that you're not telling me?"

"What?" Sulie smacked his arm. "Not me. I'm just saying that you should allow yourself to get carried away with passion once in a while."

He nodded as he studied her. "I don't remember the last time you had a date."

Her jaw hardened and a stern look came to her eyes. "Do you want my help or not?"

William knew when to drop a subject. "Jackie is here and she's wearing a gold costume with a feathered mask. You can leave when you need to, but for now, let's keep looking for her."

Jackie tossed her empty plate into the trash, along with the empty plastic wine glass. Eating five mini–cheese-cakes was foolish since Steve wasn't worthy of her time or attention, and alcohol wasn't going to solve anything either. He had made a fool of her once more. And he did so in front of their coworkers with the red slutty devil. Jackie should have known better. Pitty party or not, she never should have agreed to come here tonight with him.

She turned the light off in the music room and left her

secluded spot. The room didn't prove much of a haven since it only gave her time to think of how stupid, and how desperate, she had been. Not anymore. She planned to walk out this door, march into the gym, and give Steve a piece of her mind. She would be the one to publicly dump and humiliate him, not the other way around.

As the sound of her high heels clicked against the tiled floor of the long hallway leading back to the gym, she fumed over her poor judgment and where she was in her life. She only had a job because Steve provided one for her with his trust fund money. She had no husband and no babies—she didn't need them to define herself as a successful woman—but dammit, she wanted her happily ever after with a man who wanted to grow old with her. Was it too much to hope for?

When she entered the gym, Mr. Vampire conveniently walked past her, his black cape swaying with every step. He walked slowly around the room, as though looking for someone. Perhaps he sought the sexy red devil or another woman, but not her. Since she hadn't talked to the man since their arrival, she doubted he even noticed her absence. He was probably looking for the she-devil bombshell who had hung all over him while he signed up for the romantic dinner auction. When Jackie checked the auctions earlier, she was pleased to see someone had outbid loverboy.

She matched Steve's pace as her anger built. She wasn't going to give him the satisfaction of a scene. Oh no, he didn't seem worthy of such effort. A curt, "you're such an idiot and not worthy of my time" shake-down would suffice, with her taking the higher ground and looking repugnantly at him.

At least, that was the plan. And naturally, intentions are different from reality.

Using her index finger, she poked him in the back. "You son–of–a–bitch!" she fumed before he could turn around. Ladies from a nearby table stopped talking as Jackie's words caught their attention. "I come here with you, listening the entire drive how you've changed and I'm the only woman for you. Then you go and treat me this way? Hell no!" She swallowed the lump in her throat as she noticed which ladies now sat at the table. The gossipy witches of the admin staff at her school got an ear–full. It didn't matter. She took a deep breath and centered herself. "I only agreed to come here tonight so I could find out the truth about the grant money you gave to the school—the money you lied to me about. Since I have *you* to thank for my sorry ass job, I quit!"

She took a deep breath as she heard her own words. She hadn't planned to quit, she also didn't mean to spill the beans on where the grant money had come from. She needed this job, and her father needed her financial support. She stood taller and felt her resolve. She needed her dignity more than anything else, and her father would understand. Besides, taking control of her life felt good.

Mr. Dracula turned around, his partially covered up face now visible to her. His smooth cocoa skin color, his deep brown soulful eyes, and militarily cut hair... all foreign to her.

"I believe you have me confused with someone else," his deep voice filled the air.

Her eyes widened as she let out a gasp. This was not Steve.

CHAPTER 16

*J*ackie felt a heaviness settle in her chest. She had made a terrible mistake, and in front of the gossipy witches no less. She licked her suddenly dry lips and inhaled a deep breath. "I thought you were someone else. I'm so sorry," she squeaked out.

Even though he wore a mask, Jackie could see a trace of recognition in his deep brown eyes. A smile spread across his full lips.

"I'm not. I've been looking everywhere for you," he said.

His voice sounded deep and sinful. She took a good look at Mr. Dracula and became unsure what to say, especially in front of witnesses. She felt her heart pounding in her chest. She wasn't sure if the surprise had set it off, or the fact that this incredibly handsome man stood before her. She had no idea who he was, but she needed to find out.

Her fingers touched a curl of hair along her cheek. "You've been looking for me?" she asked coyly.

The masked man stepped and closed the gap between the two of them. He reached out and held her hand. "You're the reason I came to the party."

It was a smooth line, and even though she saw it as such, she loved hearing the words—especially since his voice rang of sincerity. She gave him a playful smile and said, "And if I had already left the party and not bumped into you?"

His free hand touched his chest. "Then I would have truly missed one of my life's greatest moments."

As cheesy as the line was, she did like the sound of it, so she smiled back at him. He was handsome, complimentary, and sexy as hell. She bit her lip as she surveyed his beautiful body. Muscles stretched the fabric of his costume, showing his pecs and broad shoulders. Even without touching him, she could tell his chest was rock hard—as well as his abs. This tall, dark, and handsome man also had a firm butt, Jackie was sure of that. Unfortunately, even if she asked him to turn around, she knew his cape would cover up the beautiful sight.

She playfully bit down even more on her lower lip as she sighed, her eyes scanning down past his abs to even more exciting body parts.

"Jackie?"

She cleared her throat and looked him squarely in the eyes. "Yes?"

"I guess you didn't hear me. I asked if you wanted to sit down?" His head tilted to the side. "Are you all right?"

A light chuckle escaped her throat. "Oh, I'm fine Mr. Vampire. Just fine."

CHAPTER 17

*J*ackie set her wine glass down on the coffee table as she removed her high heels and folded her long legs beneath her. The over-sized, stuffed couch in the teacher's lounge molded to her body, making her realize just how comfortable the old, donated furniture to the school could be.

She licked her lips as she eyed the delicious man in the vampire costume. What was it going to take to find out his identity? They had talked for such a long time. Was he really going to have her wait until midnight to find out?

What a stupid party rule, she thought. At the stroke of midnight masks come off and you reveal who you are.

Sipping another glass of wine slowly, she enjoyed Mr. Vampire's company, and bided her time. Moving their conversation into the lounge, and away from prying eyes, had been her decision—and she was grateful for the opportunity to get to know the masked man. For starters, he wore no ring on his finger. He looked hotter than Denzel Washington, spoke silkier than James Earl Jones, and had a personality sweeter than honey. For all intents and purposes, he seemed like the perfect package.

But who the hell was he?

She stared longingly at him. If she could believe what he told her, he was searching for a Mrs. Right. The idea of family and growing old with someone appealed to him. Other than her father, Jackie didn't think such men existed anymore—at least none had ever looked her way before.

The clock couldn't count down time fast enough for her to get to know who he was.

She peeked down at her watch and realized nearly an hour had passed since they had entered the room. During that time, she had confirmed he had granted the money to the school and that he somehow knew her, but she didn't know who he was.

Not having the upper hand made her a bit uneasy, but he was so easy to talk to that she put her fears to rest and opened up to him. She shared with him her heartache of not being the best art and music teacher for the school, especially since the kids deserved a whole lot more from their teacher than she could give them. Even as the words escaped her mouth, she couldn't believe she was confiding that information to him. She had suppressed the truth of her inadequacy deep down, not wanting it to come out. And now, she was opening a floodgate.

She shared her fears about her father's happiness, well-being and health next, followed by any apprehension she felt towards what direction her life was heading and how she felt powerless to take control. Jackie rolled her eyes, even her job had been a gift given to her and not something she had earned.

A job given to her by the very same masked man sitting across from her. A man whose name she didn't know.

During all the time Jackie rambled, she noticed how good of a listener this man was. How he had nodded and allowed her to lean on his shoulder, even offering bits of his own past when his stories ran parallel to hers. Through his stories, Jackie got to know her masked man. He wasn't much different from many of the boys she taught at the school who were being raised by foster parents and trying to balance responsibilities and life.

She gazed at him and felt a tingling in the pit of her stomach. He sat across the couch from her, smiling in such a way that his brown eyes reflected his thoughts and feelings. Her arm lay draped across the back of the couch, and she was pleased when he mirrored the position and softly touched her hand, caressing her skin softly with his fingers.

His hand felt cool to the touch, even though she found the room quite warm. She tugged at the neckline of her costume where sweat had beaded. Yes. It was definitely warm in here. She wasn't sure if it was the alcohol taking effect, the actual temperature of the room, or perhaps the gorgeous man sitting next to her. She gave a longing look at his full red lips and wondered if he kissed tenderly or passionately. Either way would be fine.

And even with her overt gaze, he did not make a move towards her. Why hadn't he tried to kiss her yet? She had played with her hair a countless number of times, and had even leaned in closer once or twice. She thought surely when she touched his arm once before that it would be a prelude to something, but nothing was forthcoming.

This man seemed different from the other men in her life, patient and kind. Any other man would take advantage of her alone in this room, and she was stupid even to venture in here with him, but there was something so honest about him.

Her fingers sought out his fingers on top of the couch, and she returned the soft caress doing her best to warm him. "It's nearly midnight," she said playfully.

Thank God.

He sat straighter on his side of the couch, as if Jackie had announced she was Cinderella and needed to leave the ball. "The time is still early," he protested.

"The party ends at midnight. Everyone removes their mask and the auction winners are announced."

Finally, she would find out who he was.

Smiling, he confessed, "I don't know anyone else at the party, and I don't care if I won any auctions or not." His hand now left hers on the couch and lifted to the side of his mask. "You're the only one who needs to know who I am."

He pulled the mask away, and Jackie let out a gasp. It was him. William what's-his-name, the Secret Service agent from all those months ago—the man she hadn't stopped thinking about. She had no idea it would be him, and yet, a part of her wasn't surprised to discover his true identity. Her heart raced at seeing him again.

CHAPTER 18

The feeling of butterflies erupted in Jackie's stomach when William said he wasn't quite ready to end the evening, and that he wanted to take her out.

After removing their masks, William had taken off his cape and said their outfits might be a bit showy for where he wanted to go, but that they would be passable. She at first suspected he planned to take her out dancing or to some other gracious event. But he hinted that he had something more special in mind.

The drive was a bit lengthy, but she knew her way around the city and was familiar with the streets. William then turned down Pennsylvania Avenue, and Jackie quietly smiled. She loved this street. Passing in front of the White House always had her turn her head just to get a look at the place. It was one of the perks living in D.C..

Her head was already turned to take in the lovely image, when she heard the car blinker sound as they approached the impressive home. William passed some protesters and then turned down the North Drive in front of the mansion.

Jackie's jaw dropped. "You're kidding?"

"I thought you'd like to see where I work."

She couldn't even breathe. He was taking her to the White House? My God! How cool was that? Her face now hurt with how big of a smile she now wore.

As they pulled up to the impressive mansion, Jackie's eyes grew wider in delight and she could feel her heart beating faster. "You're taking me to the White House?" she asked again.

Grinning from ear to ear, William drove onto the North Portico where guards awaited his identification. Before they reached the guard station, William stared intently at her, and for a moment Jackie thought something might be wrong.

"You don't intend to harm the President, his family, or endanger anyone within the White House, do you?"

Before she could even think, she answered, "No."

"Do you now, or have you ever, planned to take over the government."

Again, the word "no" escaped her lips. She felt slightly dizzy and realized the car was now parked along the north staircase of the White House, but she didn't remember the guard giving back the IDs. And yet, her driver's license rested safely in her hands.

She shook her head, realizing she had drunk too much wine earlier in the evening.

A guard opened her door and let her out of the car while William came around to hold out his arm before escorting her into the building.

"Have you ever been in the White House before?"

Jackie shook her head. Barely able to speak, she managed to say, "I've been meaning to go on the public tour. Just never got around to it."

She counted each step, reveling in the glory of where she was. But then something occurred to her. Halfway up the stairs, she stopped. "Are we going to be in trouble for just walking in here?"

William stopped, as well. "I work here. I'm here every day."

She stood one step higher than him and looked directly into his eyes. "But do you have any reason to be here tonight?"

He continued walking and urged her to follow. "Yes. I want to show you the White House."

She realized she had been smiling most of the evening. As far as best dates go, this was numero uno on her list.

As they made their way into the building, the swiftness with which the guards let them pass impressed Jackie. With only a few words from William, nearly a virtual red carpet was laid at their feet. She figured he stood higher up in rank in his job than she thought, or maybe these people owed him a favor, or perhaps it was just this easy to enter the White House. She hoped it wasn't the latter one.

More guards greeted them when they walked across the Grand Entrance Hall. Jackie took in her surroundings as William briefly talked with the guards.

If she had ever guessed how magnificent this home really was, she would have missed its true beauty by a mile. The reflection of the chandelier sparkled in the marble tile as they made their way towards a room across from the entrance doors. Large paintings of presidents hung on the walls, and Jackie, as a teacher, recognized each one—although she may have confused the identify of a few of them in her mind. Every last detail accounted for, including crown molding and red carpet in what William had called the Cross Hall leading to the adjoining staircase.

He paused at the open door and nodded for her to enter first. To her amazement, the room was... well, it was green. The walls, the carpet, the drapes, even the furniture were all different shades of green. It was green, but dazzlingly beautiful.

"This is the Green Room," he said, walking into the room behind her.

"Oh, I think *that's* obvious." She smiled as she walked across the room, her finger lightly touching the back of the couch as she made her way to the fireplace. The atmosphere almost didn't seem real.

She could tell he followed her by his footsteps so close behind. "There's also a Red Room, a Blue Room and a Yellow..."

"Let me guess," she interrupted. "There's a yellow room."

He chuckled. "The yellow room is upstairs. The President and his wife use it as a private den, so it's off the tour."

She walked to the window and looked outside. "I never thought of the White House having a television, or of the first family watching programs."

William now joined her at the window. "They're a normal couple, just like everyone else."

"A normal couple where the husband is the ruler of the free world." Jackie stepped back and admired the crystal chandelier in the middle of the ceiling. "You know what room I've always wanted to see? The dish room."

A smile crossed his lips. "The China Room?" When she nodded, he asked, "Why is everyone so fascinated with a bunch of plates?"

She now looked at him, a sly smile on her face. "Do you take all of your dates to the White House?"

"No." He blushed. "I mean, what dates?"

Her question made him squirm where he stood. It was a joke, and even if he didn't enjoy it, she did.

William noticed over the course of the evening how playful Jackie had become, but the question still surprised him. Other vampires of the COLONY team had taken women into this home to impress them, but Jackie was the first one for him. She was special, and even though he was a bit nervous using the allure of the majestic building to sweep her off her feet, the Green Room had a reputation for charming the ladies. Many Secret Service agents had done this move in the past, as well as Daniel, another COLONY member who had actually had sex on the couch right here in this room.

Bringing her to the White House was a silly romantic notion. The truth was, he wanted to sweep Jackie off her feet and make love to her in this historic spot. But he did not want the hassle of explaining his actions in this room to his commander Raymond, who was a much bigger and more intimidating vampire than William. Video cameras monitored this room and William didn't want that type of exposure, or to be the butt of every Green Room joke for the next decade like poor Daniel was.

Jackie stood next to him now, in this tranquil room. He watched her smile, and it looked as if she enjoyed the situation. She liked to be in control, to be in charge and have her way—and she couldn't be sexier to him. He noticed the deep breath she took, the slightest nibble she did on her lower lip, and most of all, he noticed her soft bedroom eyes as they looked up and studied his own lips.

She then leaned forward, moving only halfway so he would need to do the same.

This was it. He would finally get to kiss Ms. Jackie Pearlman. He took a deep breath and licked his dry lips. He then leaned in and was about to close his eyes. But he paused before his lips reached hers.

A small red dot danced atop Jackie's temple. He barely had time to block her from the window before the bullet shattered the glass and streaked through the room piercing him in his shoulder.

CHAPTER 19

*P*ain blasted through William's right shoulder as glass sprayed across him and Jackie as they fell to the floor. Her frightened eyes stared back at him as he lay on top of her.

"What the hell was that?" she asked.

William studied Jackie's face, and thought she seemed okay, just a bit shaken up. He didn't have much time, and definitely couldn't explain things to her right now. Not that he knew exactly what was going on.

Damn. He was in pain. It throbbed through his body, and his right arm lay limply at his side. His guessed his shoulder blade had split in two due to the massive amount of blood streaming down his side.

He was going to age in front of her if he didn't get out of the room. With this much blood loss, he may even be tempted to bite her.

Great. Now all he could was smell the blood pulsing within her veins. Shit. He needed to leave, and before the roladen shut down over the windows.

The swift hum of the window shutters became easily detectable to his sensitive ears, and he had little time before all windows of the house, as well as all public doors, were sealed in the lockdown.

"Stay here, and out of the way," he managed to grunt out. He then made a running leap through the broken window just as a steel shutter whipped downward and sealed the room off from the outside world. Next, a team of Secret Service agents armed with assault rifles scrambled into the room. That's when a second shot rang out.

The shots had come from the southern side of the building, the side facing the South Lawn and leading to the National Mall. William understood how many military snipers were on location in the area, but if he followed the scent fast enough, he could track down the shooter by the smell of gunpowder, and he wanted to find the bastard who had targeted Jackie.

But he was a black man, in somewhat of a disguise, running away from the White House after two gunshots. Regardless of what the sniper looked like, William knew that he too would be a target of those snipers. He'd have to run, and run fast.

With his vampire speed, William managed to track the shooter as he ran from the White House Basketball Court south to E Street NW. His shoulder ached and he could feel blood streaming down his back, soaking his white undershirt and the black Dracula costume. He had never been shot before, and the amount of pain surprised him. His body had the ability to heal and to expel the bullet, but only if he was at rest. With each quickened step he took, the ripped flesh of his shoulder pulled even more, causing more damage.

Human. The shooter was definitely human. The stench of him hung in the air with the gun shot residue. William licked his lips. The scent of the blood in the man's arteries now grew stronger. The man's heart rate was elevated, probably due to the run, and William could tell his prey was close by. William quickened his pace, his fangs already extending wanting his next meal, and his eyes pitching black.

But even before William caught the man, he could tell his body had aged. His speed had slowed and his body felt weaker, and he knew it wasn't just from the blood loss, but due to his body now aging decades in only a few minutes.

He was running out of time, not just because of his aging, but because the human agents would arrive in seconds. He saw the sniper running and ran to cut him off. He leapt through the air and tackled him to the ground, the two of them tumbling into some bushes.

William held the sniper tightly and forced him to make eye contact with him. "Be still and quiet."

The man had barely undergone the compulsion when William turned his prey's head to the side and dove in for what he so desperately needed.

CHAPTER 20

*J*ackie's head had hit the green oriental rug with a thud as she fell over backwards after the bullet struck. She had grasped onto William as she lost her balance, and had taken him with her to the floor—his strong body had landed atop of hers. Years had passed since she heard a gun firing, and even then, she had never been so close as to be sprayed with glass from its destruction.

As her heart pounded, she had barely heard a word William said to her, and could not process the information. She had turned her head to watch him jump out the shattered window at a super fast speed just as a sheet of metal clamped down on the window blocking her not only from the outside world but also from William.

Now, she took a deep breath and figured she must be dreaming that someone was attacking the White House. And the speed in which William took off? She surely must have exaggerated that due to the blow she took to the head. The blow she took because of... well, an attack on the White House...

God, it could be a script for a bad horror movie. What was she supposed to do next?

When a security detail entered the Green Room, she heard another shot being fired and then the room suddenly fell dark, with only a faint red light emanating from the ceiling. Soldiers surrounded her, giving her a claustrophobic feeling in the pit of her stomach. From her position on the floor, she only saw the soldiers' arsenal of guns pointing at her and infrared light from their helmets and weapons. She felt certain the second bullet had not entered this room due to the big sheets of metal that closed the windows of the room. She became aware of voices talking back and forth on walkie-talkies when a soldier leaned down and asked her to identify herself.

Everything seemed to travel in slow motion, just like when you are about to take a nasty fall. She raised her hands slowly to show them she was unarmed. "My name is Jackie, Jackie Pearlman." She tried to sit up on her own, but a guard ordered her not to do so. They asked for identification and held their guns sharply on her as she searched around for her gold clutch purse. It had hung on her shoulders and now lay several feet away near where a soldier stood on the green carpet. She watched as he picked her small bag up and nearly ripped it open to find her driver's license.

After repeatedly telling them she was a guest of William Wardell and what her own name was, she heard a confirmation from one of the soldiers wearing a headset who had confirmed her statements with the visitor guest log. She assured the men she had not been wounded, and then two soldiers grabbed her arms and helped her to her feet. Shards of glass dropped from her golden costume and fell to the floor, causing a tinkling sound over the commotion in the room. Jackie now studied the broken window, which remained on the inside of the huge metal barricade. Several panes of glass were gone and scattered on the floor where she and William had recently stood. The glass, her hands, and even her purse were tinted by the red light from the ceiling.

In the background, she could hear her name come across a walkie-talkie. The guard nodded to the two soldiers who held her, and they released their hold on her.

Her moment of relief was short lived. Two guards and the man holding the walkie-talkie marched her out of the Green Room and into the hallway, crowded with even more soldiers and men in black suits, each wearing what she now suspected were infrared headgear to see in the poor light. Not even the once sparkling chandelier reflected on the marble tiles. Everything was an eerie red.

"Where are you taking me?" she demanded. But the guards ignored her.

"I said, where are you taking me?" she asked again, her voice sounding more forceful. They ignored her once more as they led her away from the room.

She stood in the long entryway, a hallway she had been thrilled to be in only moments ago. Now her mind clouded over. Who could be shooting at the White House? And where did William disappear to? She wondered if she were safe in this building, and if she would be released by the Secret Service within any reasonable time frame.

Her gaze darted around the room. Where had all these

soldiers come from? It looked like a small city had erupted into the house.

Her body cringed. Guns. These were not little pistols, but huge weapons. There were too many rifles to count and she felt sick to her stomach. The entire world had changed with the explosive sounds of two gunshots.

Through the dim red light, she saw an elderly man in a suit quickly walking in the background. He seemed out of place, so she watched him carefully, even though no one else seemed to notice him.

The red light made it hard to see, but she thought the man wore a brown suit, which seemed odd enough, but he used his hands to cover his face. His white hair showed his age as he walked into a nearby room. The door remained opened and she could see red paint on the walls and red carpeting—or at least they looked red since the room also had the red warning lights. The mystery man had barely taken two steps in the room when he pulled out a syringe from a cabinet drawer and jabbed it into his arm.

At first, Jackie assumed he was taking drugs as the man repeated the motion three more times. She then watched as the man's white hair became darker and his stance straighter in only a matter of minutes. The man who now left what Jackie assumed to be the Red Room, appeared to be a man in his late thirties.

What the hell? Nothing made sense, and she thought she might throw-up. Her eyes were tricking her and obviously she had a concussion or was hallucinating. She couldn't have seen what she thought she had witnessed.

And yet, no one else seemed concerned. She glanced from guard to guard. She knew the military could see people better in the dark with those helmets on since they showed a thermal body heat signature of people. Why hadn't they picked him up?

The voices on the walkie–talkies brought her back to the first pressing need. Her safety and freedom. From the voices, she learned the shooter had been apprehended, and that she was to be escorted to the East Wing and interrogated.

Interrogated? What about this weirdo man injecting drugs just a few feet away? Why were these bozos not worried about *him*?

A request came over the walkie-talkie that a doctor was needed to examine her. Finally, Jackie could grasp onto something. Her mind was playing tricks on her, plain and simple. It wasn't until she heard the soldier describing her condition to the person on the other end of the line that Jackie looked down at her dress.

Why was there so much blood all over her?

CHAPTER 21

"*Y*ou don't understand!" Jackie insisted as the guards escorted her down a flight of stairs and down a darkened hallway. The same red incandescent light replaced the bright lights of the sconces, and she needed to hold onto the railing to safely follow the guards.

"William must be hurt! He was with me when the bullet broke the window." Why weren't the guards listening to her? My God, she was speaking English, wasn't she?

"William Wardell! I was with him earlier. You need to find him," she protested as they marched her across the East Colonnade. She kept pace with them, although she wanted to stop and slap them to get their attention. When they walked her past a row of windows in the East Colonnade, Jackie again saw the blacked out windows. The sight made her think of a prison lockdown.

She stopped in her tracks, the guards behind her nearly walking into her. "I'm no threat, and you need to stop wastin' your time with me." She pointed back down the hallway they had come from. "Get out there and find William!"

The guard she had assumed was in charge came up beside her. Without a word, he spun her around and placed handcuffs on her. The cold steel of the rings made her gasp as she took in the seriousness of the situation.

The guard rattled on about national security, but nothing about her right to remain silent—or any other Miranda Rights words she had heard from the television cop shows she enjoyed watching, so she assumed she wasn't being arrested.

As she thought of what to say, or even what threat to scream at them, the man in the brown suit made another appearance in this hall, but this time his attire had changed. He now wore a dark blue suit which hung loosely on him. Jackie's heart skipped a beat as he approached, his stare focused directly on her, and she felt a horror film might play out. The man appeared to be in his mid thirties, and she knew he was the same old man she had seen disappear into the Red Room. The man brushed his hand through his thick dark hair as he flashed a badge and ordered the guards to allow him to take charge of the prisoner. The term prisoner surprised her. The White House did resemble a prison currently, and she figured until she proved her innocence, they saw her as a threat. Even more disconcerting was how the guards easily allowed the mystery man to take her, as if they stood in trances and had no choice. The armed men stepped aside as though the mystery man was the President himself.

And that was the first time Jackie had thought of the

President. She suspected the man to be somewhere inside this building. What if the second bullet had killed him?

"Please remain calm and follow me." The man in the baggy blue suit ordered. Surprisingly, she felt a sudden need to walk behind him, no matter where he led her. She wanted to protest, or at least stay with the military guards, but one foot followed in front of the other back down the hallway. He led her away from all the soldiers, down a corridor to a small room on the left. No guards stood near the door, and panic surged within her. She wanted to scream, but her feet just kept moving into the room. The room contained a desk, a table and chairs, and a couch. It seemed to be someone's office, but no family pictures rested on the desk and she had never heard of the COLONY, which was the name on the emblem posted on the wall.

"You will wait here, and you will remain calm." He reached down and snapped the handcuffs from her, leaving them as twisted metal rings on the desk. He then turned to leave the room, with Jackie blankly unconcerned about the state of the handcuffs, but grateful he didn't harm her in any way. But as he began to leave, she noticed a dark stain on his white shirt. The dark colored mark stained the inside of the shirt, since it looked as if the material had soaked through. The color looked dark, like blood.

As he left the room, a woman entered the threshold of the door. Her voice sounded labored as if she had been running or very busy during the entire turmoil. "Raymond, are you okay?"

"I'm fine." He gestured with his hand to brush her off, but she appeared concerned.

"You took the second one?" She eyed him from head to toe, her gaze stopping on his chest.

"I'm fine," he reassured her as his hand lightly touched his shirt. "He got me as I ran a perimeter check of the grounds. The wound is nearly healed. What about the President and First Lady?"

"I gave them a full medical exam. Both were asleep when the attack happened, same with their daughter. They're fine." She looked into the room, and Jackie saw the woman studying her. "Is she the woman Secret Service wanted me to examine?"

"Yes. She was being escorted to the East Wing before I intercepted her." Raymond walked through the doorway, taking the new arrival with him. With the door ajar, Jackie could hear some of their conversation.

"I suspect William is cleaning up from the first hit," Raymond said.

"He took the first one?"

"I believe so. This woman's name is Jackie Pearlman. William signed her into the White House a short while ago, and I caught it on the security feed. She is covered in his blood."

"It does smell like it. Does William need my help?"

"No. Through the com chatter, I heard that William subdued the sniper. I think William took care of things in the field since one report commented on some blood on the man's neck. He is in custody and cooperating nicely with the authorities."

"And what about the attack?" the woman asked.

"The attack appears to be random. There are some protesters outside. We'll get to the bottom of it, but I don't think there is much more."

There was a slight pause, and Jackie wondered if the woman had left. Just then she heard Raymond mention the woman's name.

"Sulie, this is William's mess. I'll be helping interrogate the sniper, so I'd appreciate it if you'd help William deal with this woman."

Jackie listened intently, and finally heard the woman say, "Not to worry. If needed, I'll take care of Ms. Pearlman."

Jackie scanned the room. Yes, this was the White House and not some Turkish prison, but she wasn't sure what the woman named Sulie had in mind by "taking care" of her. No windows, and no other way out of the room existed, except the main door—which Raymond blocked.

She dashed over to the desk and tried to open some drawers, but all remained locked. Her gaze darted across the room and she noticed blood stains on a wastebasket. Gathering her resolve, she looked into the metal can and discovered a bloody brown suit, ripped and discarded. A suit she recognized all too well.

Her heart raced, and her mouth went dry as Sulie now entered the room. She was in cahoots with the mysterious man named Raymond who changed his age, so whatever this was, it wasn't good. Jackie's hand gently touched her forehead. Crazy thoughts raced in her mind. Was she even able to judge what she was seeing and hearing? Overall, she felt fine—just a small bump on the back of her head, but any head injury should be taken seriously.

Sulie wore a tailored gray suit with a white button-down shirt and her hair firmly secured in a bun, but Jackie did not see a weapon on her as she entered the tiny room.

"Jackie," the woman said softly. "Please have a seat." Her hand gestured to the couch.

Jackie's voice cracked, but she stood her ground. "I think I'd rather stand."

Sulie smiled. "You may be here awhile." Jackie noticed the woman staring intently at her, but then a few moments must have passed, because Jackie found both of them seated on the couch, with Sulie smiling at her. The woman stood. "You're physically healthy, Jackie, with only a bump on the head." She walked to the desk and leaned over to retrieve a bottle of water from the case on the floor. "You may be here awhile." She handed the bottle to Jackie and then went to the door. Taking one last look at Jackie, she said, "Stay here. Be kind to William, and listen to what he has to tell you. He's one of the good guys."

Jackie wasn't sure what happened, but she had no wish to leave the room.

CHAPTER 22

*W*illiam didn't have enough time to clean the sniper's neck by the time the human Secret Service arrived. He flashed his badge and compelled the humans to take over interrogating the perp. Not only had William compelled the sniper to comply, he seemed eager to talk.

The man rambled about white supremacy, and protested the bill the President planned to either sign or veto shortly. After pulling some strings and compelling a congressman or two, William had slipped Jackie's school funding requirements of her petition into that bill. The additional money needed would be covered, and he hoped the administration, which had done so poorly addressing education and racial unrest, would sign the bill. He now felt responsible for Jackie being the target of tonight's attack.

William took a deep breath as he helped the Secret Service march the sniper to a secure location. The man didn't know anything about Jackie. He had wanted to kill the President, but couldn't keep himself from shooting at a black woman standing in the window frame of the White House.

Gritting his teeth, William regretted that racial hatred still existed. It wasn't as prevalent as in the 1960's when he was killed as a Freedom Rider in Alabama, but it was still very much alive today. He looked at the man as guards placed him into a police car that would take him to an undisclosed location. Hate consumed the man with something as unimportant as the color of their skin. William wondered what the man would think if he hadn't been compelled to forget that a vampire, a different species, had fed on him only moments ago.

As William grinned trying to guess what the man's reaction might be, his superior, Raymond, appeared—and he didn't look happy. From the scent of blood in the air, and the fact that Raymond looked younger now than he did earlier in the day, William knew he had taken the second bullet.

Raymond pulled William aside. He studied William, looking for injuries. "Where were you hit, and were there witnesses before or after you fed?"

William filled in the details to his superior, feeling silly to have taken a date to the White House. The home was off–limits, even if many people did it.

"This house isn't your personal home, nor is it a hotel," he said sternly.

"Understood, sir." He noticed Raymond rub his chest. "Were you hit…"

"Yes, right in the chest while doing a routine perimeter check. I had aged so quickly I barely had time to get to a blood stash." Raymond now glanced at William's wounds.

"Mine was a through and through. Were you able to recover your bullet?"

William reached into a small side pocket of his costume and handed the bullet to Raymond. It had mushroomed and split into two pieces from the impact, and hurt like hell on its way out. "We also have his firearm and extra ammo."

"It's a large caliber," Raymond commented. "Looks like 50mm."

"And there's something special about the way it's made. This slug easily sliced through the bullet proof glass. The glass took most of the impact, or it would have torn my arm off."

"Thank goodness for that," Raymond said as he pocketed the slug.

William shifted from one foot to the other, wondering how much longer the debriefing would take. He wasn't sure where Jackie was, but knew she had been detained in the White House during its lockdown. William then noticed Raymond's concentrated stare.

"The woman is in Dixon's office," Raymond said.

Nodding, William knew their director was out of the city at the moment. His office remained vacant and was the perfect spot to hold Jackie while he did his best to explain things to her.

"She's confused," Raymond added.

William understood how Raymond's mental gift worked. Not all vampires had such special gifts, but Raymond's family line had been blessed by them, and they came in handy. Raymond had read Jackie's mental patterns.

Raymond tapped the com unit in his ear. "Sulie just

finished examining her. She's fine, but like I said, she's confused."

William nodded. As Raymond's sister, Sulie also had a gift and could medically examine someone just by touching them. It made sense that someone would be confused in the middle of an attack on the White House, especially since he had disappeared immediately and hadn't been seen since.

He wasn't sure what to say next, or if he was excused to leave. He wanted to check on Jackie but Raymond studied him, concentrating deeply with his eyebrows furrowed. That's when William knew the vampire was reading not just his mental patterns, but also his mind. He went with it.

Raymond's scowl disappeared, and his facial expression softened. "This is the woman you mentioned to me a few months ago?"

"Yes. She is."

"You need to clean this up with Jackie," Raymond said. "One way or the other. Do you understand?"

"I know."

"Sulie is there to help... if needed."

William took a deep breath and nodded. He walked back towards the main house and prayed Jackie would be open minded.

CHAPTER 23

William stood outside of the White House COLONY office. He knew Jackie remained safely locked away from all the chaos from the sniper. She was the woman of his dreams; he just hoped this conversation didn't turn into a nightmare.

Raymond had handed William the keys to the office before rushing out to interrogate the prisoner. William held the door key in his hand, but still knocked. He wasn't sure why, it just seemed more polite to do so. He used the key and slowly entered, saying her name as he did so.

Jackie sprang from the couch and ran towards him, engulfing him in a tight hug.

"I got so scared," she said. "I had no idea what happened, where you were,… or…"

Hearing her elevated heart rate, he tried to comfort her, but she pulled away from him as he closed the door. Her eyes focused on her wet stained hands. When her eyes grew wide in fright, he figured she realized what the stain meant.

"You've been shot!" She studied him from head to toe, but then she had a confused look on her face when he appeared healthy.

"I'm fine," he insisted. He took a quick glance at the video camera in the corner of the room. The red record light glowed. Since vampires used this room for feeding, the monitor gave the human Secret Service a fake video feed. His head leaned to the side, questioning the red light he saw. The light blinked off and back on twice, telling him live footage was being transmitted—and he knew to whom. Sulie was watching everything unfold, ready to jump in and help him clean up a potential mess with Jackie.

William could compel Jackie to forget everything, but history had proven he usually hesitated in such matters— unnecessarily terrifying the woman even more. The last thing he wanted was for her to run from him in a panic and get caught up in the disarray outside.

He motioned to the couch. "Please sit down."

Her body went rigid. "You have gray in your hair," she gasped. Backing away from him, she pointed to his aged face.

William cursed inwardly. Maintaining his age to the exact year proved difficult. Not only was there gray in his hair, but he was certain wrinkles had formed around his eyes as well. "I can explain."

Jackie backed farther away. An explanation existed for all of this. *Space aliens.* He belonged to an alien race come here to kill the President. The idea sounded crazy, but what else could it be?

He took a seat on the couch, sitting as far from her as possible with his hands folded in his lap, trying to look as unthreatening as possible. She appreciated his efforts, although she remained ready to run to the door if needed —even if she didn't make it out of the room, she could scream bloody murder.

He let out a sigh, and Jackie thought he seemed nervous. "You believe in equality for all, and I'm a member of a very small minority. One whose numbers are only in the thousands."

It must have been a large mother ship they came in on, she thought.

"Several of us protect the President." He now looked up at the COLONY emblem on the wall behind the desk. "Council Of Legalized Outlanders for National securitY."

She studied the letters. The round seal had the United States across the top, the word COLONY on the bottom, with an eagle atop a shield with thirteen stars circling it.

"The COLONY," she read. "Shouldn't the acronym be COLONS?" It seemed fitting as she suspected he'd be shoveling a load of BS her way.

"No," he said, chuckling. "We are a select group, and at the time of our team's creation several colonies still existed around the world. There were British colonies and even American Indian reservations, which were like colonies unto themselves. We were always just called 'the colony' without any real description as to who we were. Eventually, someone filled in the acronym for us."

"Several of you are here in the White House?"

He cleared his throat. "We work wherever the President works."

She noticed him glance up towards the camera. The telltale red light shone brightly. "Who's watching us?"

"A team member."

She took a deep breath and tried to remember the names she had heard earlier. "Which one? Sulie or Raymond?"

His eyes widened. "Sulie. She is a good friend of mine. She even came to the party with me earlier tonight."

Jackie thought of the beautiful blonde and pieced the story together. She closed her eyes and sighed, unable to believe how stupid she had been. "Sulie was *your* date." Jackie felt like a fool, but also sensed the heaviness of guilt weighing in on her. Sulie must have been the sexy devil from earlier in the evening. Her style was now all prim and proper with a severe bun while she worked at the White House, but it was her earlier at the party.

"Sulie wasn't my date. She was helping me find you."

Jackie gasped and her hand went to her lips. "I made a terrible mistake." When Wiliam paused and stared at her, she added, "Steve was dressed in the same costume as you. I thought he was making time with her."

She saw the pained expression in William's eyes. "I know you have feelings for him, and I'm so sorry, but he did hit on Sulie and another woman tonight."

Jackie waved her hand dismissively. Puh-lease! She didn't care about Steve; it only bothered her that she had prejudged him. She preached to people about giving everyone a fair shake, and she was acting like a fool. She now looked at William. Was she doing the same with him?

She took a deep breath. Whatever the truth was, she wanted to hear it. "Tell me everything," she said.

"I'm immortal."

Yeah, right.

"A vampire," he clarified.

She wasn't sure if she wanted to laugh, cry or scream —so she went with the obvious comment. "You were *dressed* as a vampire earlier tonight."

He glanced down at his outfit. "A sick joke. Sulie rented the costume for me."

Jackie realized she was holding her breath, and her hand rested on her neck. "And, as a vampire, you bite people."

"No. Well, yes. Sometimes, when necessary. I inject blood from syringes into my veins because it's easier to do than drinking blood and having my spleen move it from my digestive tract to my circulatory system." He sighed, and then continued. "We can't produce blood, so we need human blood to circulate in our veins. The older the blood is, like the oil of a car, the more circulated it becomes. The blood slowly thickens, changing from red to purple, then to a dark black. Eventually, the blood becomes almost tar-like. Our cells age the older and more recycled the blood is."

Jackie had wanted the answers as to why Raymond's age had changed. She shook off her fear, realizing she should be careful what she wished for. She felt her heart pound. Could William hear it?

"Take a deep breath and calm down," he suggested.

"Don't you be telling me what to do!" she blurted out, upset he could tell how nervous she had become. She planned to wrap this knowledge around her mind if it was the last thing she did. At least, she knew where to begin with her questions.

"That man, Raymond," she said. "I saw him age."

William nodded. "He took the second bullet through the heart."

"So he's old one minute, and the next minute he's young?"

"Pretty much."

"And he was shot through the heart, but didn't die?"

In a soft voice, William answered, "Yes."

She sucked in a deep breath and let it out slowly. "I was the only one who noticed him. Can you be invisible?"

"What? No."

He looked confused, so Jackie explained how none of the soldiers saw Raymond earlier.

William shrugged. "We're predatory creatures, blending into the background. We also don't have body warmth for the scanners they wore. I guess that's how Raymond went unnoticed."

He held up his hand and offered it to her for examination, but she shook her head, not wanting to touch him. Although it did make sense why his fingers were cold earlier.

"So," she said, gathering her thoughts and pointing to his hair. "You aged tonight."

"Decades. But I... fed and took care of things."

"Syringes?"

He shook his head. "Neck."

Jackie bit her lower lip and took a deep breath. "Who did you kill?"

His eyes quickly widened. "I don't kill people to feed. I guess some vampires might, but the COLONY members all took oaths not to kill or compel anyone—well, unless necessary. I fed from the sniper. He's alive and being interrogated by Raymond right now."

Wait a minute. Compel? She did not like the sound of that. "Did you ever compel me?"

He swallowed the lump in his throat. "I compelled you in the line of duty, to make sure I could bring you to this house. I then compelled the guards to let us in without any complications."

Of course. The time–lapse she experienced and the ease in which they walked through the most protected home in America now made sense. She could see why a sworn and devoted team of vampires would be useful to protect the President. If a vampire wanted to gain access, would anyone be able to stop them?

She looked at William. He sat upright, not allowing his body to touch the back of the couch. He seemed uncom-fortable.

"You were shot in the back," she said.

"My shoulder. I'm healed now. Just one of the perks of being turned."

"When were you…"

"The 1960s."

Holy crap! He was nearly her father's age. "Who turned you?"

"Another COLONY agent, not Raymond or Sulie."

"And *they* had been turned."

He shook his head. "No. Raymond and his sister Sulie were born vampires. We *can* have our own babies."

Born? Not turned? It was so much to wrap her mind around. One thing was certain, though, William had died at some point to be turned. "How did you die?" she asked with a softened tone in her voice.

"I rode a bus to Alabama; me and many others did it to protest racial inequality. A riot broke out, as they often did back in the day. Before I knew it, I had taken a bad blow to the head." He touched the back of his skull. "One of my team members, Ben, turned me."

A gasp left her throat. A Freedom Rider. My God. She had read about them in her history text books. Her father had told her stories. William had lived through all of that.

William lifted his hands and slowly stood. She flinched and scooted farther away on the couch.

"If you don't mind," he said, "I'd like to change into a clean shirt. The director keeps clean clothes in his office."

Never taking her eyes off him, she allowed him to cross the room to the locked desk. Using a key, she saw him take out a white T–shirt from the top drawer. He lifted his blood soaked costume from his chest, revealing a soiled white T–shirt that was stained nearly black. The costume barely hung by a thread on his muscular form, and the white T–shirt had a big hole in the back, so he tore it from his body.

And what an amazing body it was. Like he had been chiseled out of marble.

She stood and walked to him, touching him gently on his sticky back. Her hand traveled gracefully down his muscular body, her fingers dancing across his powerful, well muscled form. He turned towards her, and now her hand gently caressed his chest. She felt his muscles grow tense under her fingertips.

He felt human.

"Could you have died tonight?" she asked.

His square jaw tensed visibly. "It's always a possibility. We're immortal, but only as long as we have human blood circulating in our bodies."

He looked powerful, his stained chest broad and muscular with no scars or wounds. "Why did the sniper attack the White House?"

"Raymond will get the entire story, but the sniper mentioned something about the bill the President is to sign. I put your petition allowing the funding to be granted once again to inner city schools into that bill. He was one of the protesters outside but decided to use deadly force to get his point across by killing the President—that is, until he saw a black person at the window. He thought it was more in line with the point he was trying to make."

Jackie grimaced at the thought. William could have died, and the only reason he came to the White House was because of their date. He had stood at that window because she was the one who was looking out of it. "He wanted to kill you."

William gazed into her eyes. "No. The red tracking laser was on *your* temple."

CHAPTER 24

*J*ackie's heart sank. "Red laser?"

He touched her head where evidently he had seen the tracker. "There was only a chance that I would die, but you would have died instantly. I couldn't let that happen."

Her mind raced. A red dot had targeted her. She would have been dead. Not William, but *her*. Her knees gave way, and William caught her as she sank towards the floor. He placed her gently on the couch, but one thing repeatedly came to her mind. She would be dead.

Dead—if it weren't for William.

The air seemed to have left the room, for she couldn't breathe. She felt tears trickle down her cheeks as she tried to catch her breath.

"Try to relax, Jackie." William used the soft t–shirt in his hand to brush the tears from her cheeks.

His hands felt cold to her, but she didn't care. She reached for him, needing to have him hold her. She noticed she was trembling.

"You're fine. I wasn't going to let anything happen to you." He gently held her hand up to his lips and kissed her palm. "You're fine."

She stared at her savior, grateful for what he had done. When he smiled back at her, she realized it wasn't gratitude she now felt. It was as though she now understood how the Grinch's heart had grown three sizes in just a moment in that children's cartoon, for certainly hers had grown tenfold for William and what he had done to save her.

He was a good man, and the start of feelings she had for him had nothing to do with reason. He was a strong and brave man, uh, vampire. He wanted the same things in life she wanted. In every way, the two of them matched.

Suddenly, she felt choked up, and she knew she was willing to explore a relationship where she could open herself to someone completely. For all she knew, he could very well be The One for her. Only time would tell.

She saw the concern in his eyes, felt the tenderness of his touch, and saw his lean hips and firm build as he sat next to her on the couch. She bit her lower lip, taking in how gorgeous he was. Knowing what was in her heart, there was only one thing to do.

"William," she said in a softened tone. "Catch me."

His hands went out. "You're already lying down."

Tears filled her eyes. "No. I'm going to take a leap for love, and I need you to catch me."

Jackie's beautiful features held a certain sensuality as she gazed into his eyes. William leaned in and lightly brushed a curl of her hair back from her forehead, just at the spot where he nearly lost her. He nervously licked his parched lips and gently kissed her.

Her hands captured the nape of his neck, her fingers tugging at his short military haircut as she kissed him back. The kiss started slow and thoughtful, but soon became fueled by desire. She moaned as he applied more pressure.

William took a quick glimpse at the camera. The red light was off, allowing them privacy. With the door still locked, he knew no one would come in.

Wrapping his arms around her midriff, he moved his body atop hers, easing her farther back onto the plush couch. His fingers found the row of buttons on her costume and quickly undid the first few, allowing a sexy black bra to show. He eased the lacy cup of the garment aside, revealing a taut perky nipple.

He noted that she arched her back as his tongue teased her hardened flesh. Tugging at the costume, he exposed the second beautiful mound and gave it equal time.

His fangs extended, but he resisted the temptation to nibble down her slender waist as he unbuttoned even more of the costume. With the last batch of buttons undone, the opened dress now revealed something a bit odd to him. He expected her underwear to match the bra, or at least be some type of sexy garment. Instead, she wore a somewhat large, full cotton panty.

Jackie quickly sat up, her hands grabbing the sides of the dress and covering herself up. Her beautiful face, which looked lovely to him all flushed with blood, showed what he guessed was embarrassment.

"Insurance policy," she said.

Looking away from the white bloomers, his eyes sought her's. His eyebrow rose in question. "Insurance policy?"

Her hands covered her mouth as she let out a gasp, her body going rigid. "Your eyes are black!"

Sitting up, he lifted his strong body from hers. "They blacken like this," he said as he looked away from her, "during heightened emotions." His swollen manhood pressed against the pants of his costume as he shifted his body from her.

"Let me see."

He hesitated slightly, and made sure to cover his fangs with his lips before looking her straight in the eyes. Her facial expression was more curiosity than fear, which he took as a good sign. After a moment of gazing into her eyes, she said, "They look like ebony pearls."

Her response sounded like music to his ears. At least she wasn't screaming. Swallowing the lump in his throat, he asked, "So you don't mind that I'm different?"

She let out a sigh and he felt her eyes heavily on him as she pondered his question.

"There is nothing wrong with being different." Her hand sought out his thigh and she gently stroked his leg. "Cold to the touch and ebony eyes." She scooted closer to him on the couch. "Do you have fangs?"

Never before had he felt so bare and exposed in front of a woman, not even when naked and having sex with them. In the past, when he would bite a woman, he would erase what he was from their memory afterwards since it always allowed his relationships to last longer that way. He didn't want to risk ending whatever he could have with Jackie by scaring her. "I won't bite you."

William checked the sound of her heart. It beat quickly, but he smelled the arousal that pooled between her legs, and doubted the response of her quickened heart was because of fear. Her hand searched farther up his leg, across his inner thigh, and pressed him firmly between his legs. His body stiffened as he let out a moan, showing his fangs.

Her eyebrows rose with curiosity at the sight of the incisors, but at least she didn't panic. He suppressed the urge to cover them, and allowed her to examine him. For what seemed like several minutes, she stared into his mouth and seemed excited by her discovery.

A wry smile crossed her lips. "I'm going to lay down some ground rules," she announced.

Ground rules sounded pretty good, especially since her hand still gripped him tightly.

"I don't want to be turned into a vampire, so you are not allowed to bite me."

"Biting someone doesn't automatically turn…"

Her hand raised and she stopped him mid sentence. "No biting—at all."

Her hand rubbed his swollen member, as if that would convince him to agree to whatever she would say.

"Damn, woman. You just take control, don't you?" He shifted his hips to enjoy more of her. "No biting. I swear."

"Next," she continued as she leaned in to whisper in his ear, "I want to go into this fully aware of what you are."

"Uh, huh," he said nodding.

"You're going to strip for me."

CHAPTER 25

*J*ackie released her firm grip on William's manhood, disappointed to let go of the bulging rod. But as she sat back on the couch, she knew she'd see him in his full glory in just a moment.

William stood in front of the couch. He balanced himself as he stood, looking as if he'd lose control of his passion at any moment.

"I'm sorry there's no music," he said breathlessly.

"It's okay. A good strip tease doesn't need music." Her gaze traveled across his already bare chest. "I know you have no body heat, fangs and beautiful, black eyes." Thinking back to earlier and his jump through the shattered window, she added, "You can also move at fast speeds. Show me the rest 'cuz I want to know what I'm getting myself into."

His hands unbuckled his belt, and he slowly pulled the long leather strap from the black costume pants. He then placed it onto the desk.

"Don't put that too far away," Jackie said extending her hand. "It may be useful."

He smiled as he fetched the belt and handed it to her. He then placed his hand on the button of the pants. "I'm a mess," he said, looking down at his bloodstained chest.

She stared at his chest, this time not at his ripped muscles. Her eyes focused on the dried blood covering him, which was the battle wound he carried from saving her. She felt the onslaught of tears welling up in her eyes, but she held them back. She'd wanted to make love to him, and it didn't matter that he wasn't shower fresh.

"I can see you just fine," she choked out.

He looked down once again at his soiled body. The darkened stains were mostly on his right shoulder and chest. Jackie suspected the blood bothered him more than it did her.

"If it bothers you…" she stood from the couch and walked to him with her half-full bottled water in her hand. Her dress fell open in the front as she crossed the tiny room, revealing her half naked body to him. "I can always rinse you off."

She opened the bottle and poured the water slowly across his body, allowing the water to drip down his broad shoulders, down his pecs and to his abs—pooling in his navel. Using the t-shirt he had left on the couch, she sensuously scrubbed him clean as best she could. When she was done with that bottle, she reached down under the desk and fetched another one from the case.

Before she opened the second bottle, he pulled the bottom drawer of the desk open and grabbed a gym bag. Inside, he found a couple of towels. "The director likes to work out," he explained as he handed the bigger towel to her and used the smaller one to stand on so no water dripped to the floor.

Jackie began pouring the second bottle over him and her arousal grew as water dripped off his taut muscles. She pressed her legs tightly together as she felt every nerve ending between her legs, unsure which was hotter —the man's incredible body, or the fact he didn't want to mess up the floor. She suspected that if any mess did occur, he would clean up after himself. He probably knew his way around a mop too, or at least a vacuum cleaner. It didn't make sense that she'd be attracted to a man who could do housework, but Lordy, it pushed all of her buttons.

As she worked her hands and the towel over his abs, he put his hands on her gold costume. "I'm also stronger than a human." With that, he ripped the costume off her shoulders and pulled the remains from her near naked body. "I thought you might want to know that," he added as he tugged the straps of her lacy bra down. His arm encircled her waist and she felt his fingers struggle with the clasp.

Holding the towel and bottle in one had, she undid the bra in a quick snap, allowing it to fall to the floor. "Stronger is good." She now put her finger on the button of his costume pants. "Show me again how strong you are."

He popped the button of his pants and it flew through the air. He then ripped the zipper down, exposing his throbbing rod, which rose past the waistline of his stretched boxer briefs. She had only gotten a peek, but her heart raced at the sight.

"I believe the blood may have dripped even lower." His

deepened black eyes glanced at the towel. "Would you mind cleaning the rest of me?"

Still enjoying the sight of him poking out from his unzipped pants, she reached for another bottle of water. "I think we'll need a lot of water to cover you sufficiently."

The pants were torn across the legs and he easily ripped them off, much like a stripper. With only his underwear on, she thought he looked better than any Calvin Klein commercial she had ever seen.

Jackie bit down on her lower lip, the anticipation killing her.

She bent down low, kneeling on the ground as she washed his thick upper thighs. Less blood had pooled there, and the makeshift sponge bath was nearly done.

In one quick motion, William ripped the remaining scrap of clothing off his body, leaving himself completely open and visibly throbbing for Jackie's touch.

She had never seen such a beautiful man before. She took her wet hand and grasped him firmly, enjoying the girth and strength she felt.

His breath hitched as she washed down the shaft of his manhood, making sure he was clean, although no bloodstain was this far south and central. His skin felt velvety smooth under her touch, and she wanted to over-power his passion. Leaning forward, she licked the hood of his shaft and was about to welcome him into her mouth.

His hand stopped her. "No, baby. Not for our first time together." His voice had deepened, and there was a rushed tone in his voice.

She had never known a man that didn't prefer the moment to be all about them, and she found the thought endearing. "You forgot one difference between you and a normal man," she said as she stood.

He took in a deep breath. "What's that?"

"You're more handsome." Her gaze traveled south. "You're also," she paused to lick her lips, "much larger."

Her need to feel him inside of her intensified. She no longer cared that she wore granny panties and had not shaved her legs. She wanted him. Right here, right now. Her hands slipped the bloomers off her body just before he scooped her up in his arms and carried her to the couch.

CHAPTER 26

*H*e lay down with her on the couch, her bare ebony skin slightly lighter than his own. Her long willowy legs had parted, so he placed one across the back of the couch and the other on the floor as he made room for himself on the plush piece of furniture. Unable to contain himself any longer, and smelling her pooled arousal, he lay on top of her and slowly entered her. Her moist folds eagerly accepted him, and a soft moan escaped her lips as he seated himself deeply within her. He felt her muscles grip tightly as he stretched her out.

Humans tended to be physically weaker than vampires, but her firm body matched his rhythm as he pressed himself into her all the way to his hilt.

With each thrust, he eased himself out and pumped her harder and harder. Her body urged him on by arching sharply, allowing his hands to cup under her and hold her bottom firmly. He rode her, even past her first orgasm of the evening.

She pulled her legs up, encircling his hips as she

screamed out his name repeatedly. He suspected months had past since another man had loved her this intensely, if ever. With that thought, his already extended fangs ached for her blood, and he forced his lips shut to prevent an accidental biting.

He was rounding the corner and nearly climaxing when he wanted to bite her again, but controlled the urge. When he heard her screaming even louder, he wondered if the guards would be pounding on the door, but he didn't care. To hear Jackie cry out for more and for him to go faster would be worth compelling the entire Secret Service.

"Bite me," she growled through several labored breaths. "I can tell you want you to. Just don't turn me."

She turned her head, exposing her neck to him. His fangs hungered for her blood, to mark her as his. They sank into her neck just as he climaxed. He drew from her neck as his seed spread within her—her body tightening with her second orgasm of the evening.

As her heart rate slowed down, and as soon as he could catch his breath, he sealed the love bite and then gazed deeply into her beautiful bedroom eyes. He knew he would want to make love to her every day for the rest of their lives.

EPILOGUE

"*A*nd? What happened after William told you the truth about him being a vampire?" Alex asked, bringing both Jackie and William back into the present.

Jackie glanced at William, who had also omitted the details of what had happened on that couch all those years ago. She winked at her husband. "Girl, you can guess the rest. And here we are, years later with three kids and still happily married.

"So the little insurance policy you had set up worked?" Alex said, giggling.

With a full laugh, Jackie replied, "Now, I know I'm not the only woman who uses granny panties and unshaven legs as a way of guaranteeing nothing sexual will happen on a date."

"I actually didn't know women did that." William smiled. "Like bristly legs would have kept me from you."

"So, something *did* happen on that couch," Alex suggested. "And Jackie is now a turned vampire."

"He was worth the risk. My feelings for him grew

every day, and before I knew it, I was in love with the man."

William glanced at Jackie. "I said the words first though."

Jackie playfully punched him in the arm. "You said those words very early in our relationship. It was during a carriage ride just before you watched me eat dinner at that nice country club." She winked at Alex. "I had him earn it before I would say I loved him."

"You didn't have me wait that long," he protested. "We got married six months later."

"Sinclair came nearly a year after that; then we had Nicole. I asked William to turn me when Sulie diagnosed me with early stage ovarian cancer a few years ago." She sighed as she looked at William. "I love this man too much to leave him. Our vows are for eternity."

Alex finished her glass of wine and set it down. "Your story is lovely, and I'm sure my husband was upset about your first date at the White House. He's such a stickler for protocol."

William hung the last of the ten finished costumes on a hanger and placed the outfit next to the others on the door handle. "Well, if not for us standing at that window, we never would have known about those special bullets. The glass in all the window panes was changed soon afterwards. We may have even saved the President's life that night, so Raymond let the indiscretion drop."

Alex's phone buzzed. "Speaking of the devil. Raymond is calling from Oregon." She stood from the kitchen table and made her way to the door, waving good night to Jackie and William. "Hi honey," she said into the phone as she closed the door to the apartment behind her.

The time was getting late, so William began cleaning the kitchen as Jackie put the sewing machine away. Their baby would get up sometime soon, and any quiet moment alone was to be cherished. Jackie had made a leap for love and as far as either of them could tell, they were both still up on cloud nine.

THE END

Please leave a review for "Equality of Service," previously known as "William's Tale." Please visit http://www.reginamorris.com/colony_4_equality_of_service to be taken to a page on the author's website that has links to all retailers that sell the book.

Find out what happens in the COLONY #5 novel, Reliant Service. Please visit http://www.reginamorris.com/colony_5_reliant_service

Want to get a sneak peek on upcoming COLONY books? You can download a FREE ebook ("Power of Four") that has the first four chapters of the first four books by visiting http://www.reginamorris.com/power-of-four-info

ABOUT THE AUTHOR

Dear Readers,

I hope you enjoyed reading my novel, **Equality of Service** *(Book #4 of the COLONY Series).*

Reviews are SO important to authors, especially independent authors such as myself. I do read them. Please do me the favor of leaving a review by visiting http://www.reginamorris.com/colony_4_equality_of_service and finding the retailer from where you purchased the book. Thank You!

You can also visit this site (http://www.reginamorris.com/retailers) to purchase additional books in the series.

Please visit my website http://www.reginamorris.com and my Facebook fan page (http://www.facebook.com/ReginaAnnMorris) for more information about the other novels in the COLONY Series. Feel free to contact me through my website, through my social media sites (see my website for the list) or by email at regina@reginamorris.com.

I live in Austin, Texas with my husband and two children. I graduated high school in Germany and I attended the University of Texas at Austin, where I received a degree in Computer Science with a minor in math. After enjoying a career in software engineering, I discovered that writing is in my blood, and had to put pen to paper!

The opinions I express in my novels are my own. My stories are my own intellectual property. Copyright (c) 2012-2020, Regina Morris

Sincerely,
Regina Morris

ACKNOWLEDGMENTS

Special thanks to my husband and our children for their love and support; to my sister for believing in me and encouraging me to follow my dream.

Many people have helped me in the creation of this novel. Special thanks to:

My Beta Readers: Lynn W. of the Paranormal Romance Guild

My Content Editor: Selena W. and Chelle L. of Literally Addicted to Detail

My Line Editor: Sue M.

My Proof Readers: Pennie B, Jean G., Rorie S, and Deb T.

I'd also like to thank my Street Team of supporters – For the Love of Fiction Team and The COLONY Street Team.

The support you have given me gave me the courage, strength and resources to complete this novel. Thank you!

ALSO BY REGINA MORRIS

BOOKS IN THE "COLONY" SERIES

Vampires exist among us. They can be our neighbor, our best friend, our child's teacher…

They alter their aged appearance based upon the amount of blood they consume. They move to a new area, drink a lot of blood, and appear young. Slowly they limit their intake of blood and age, right in front of our unsuspecting eyes. After decades, they fake their death, move, and do it over and over again.

Most live quiet lives in an effort to blend in.

Some, however, want power and control.

The COLONY is an elite group of vampires sworn to protect the President of the United States from these rogue vampires. Few humans are privileged to this knowledge.

Eternal Service (Book #1)

Amazon Top 100 Bestseller

978–0–9888222–0–7 (ebook)

978–0–9888222–1–4 (paperback)

Available as an audio book.

Vampire Raymond Metcalf has too many balls to juggle and life is getting more complicated by the minute. As if working with a covert team of sexy vampires to protect the President isn't enough, he has to deal with his rebellious half-breed son, save the President from a crazed vampire, and break in a new director for his team since the last one, his best friend and the only human he trusts, has decided to retire. Why does his friend's replacement have to be the most beautiful human woman Raymond has ever seen?

Career military woman, Alex Brennan, is being offered the promotion of a lifetime, and with it a romance that she has desperately been seeking. Does she dare accept the position as Director of the COLONY, an elite group of deadly creatures of the night and risk a dangerous romance with a man who isn't even human? Together, can they save the President?

United Service (Book #2)

Amazon Top 100 Bestseller

978−0−9888222−6−9 (ebook)

978−0−9888222−7−6 (paperback)

Available as an audio book.

Sterling Metcalf is a modern−day vampire who clashes with his father's antiquated ideals. Being the half−breed of the COLONY group, Sterling hates being the team's weakest link. He jumps at an opportunity to do some fieldwork rescuing kidnapped vampire children and is accompanied by Kate Spencer, the nanny of one of the children.

Kate is a purebred vampire with a secret of her own. Can Sterling put aside his bad−boy ways and woo the lovely Kate? Will Kate accept the advances of a half−breed? Together, can they save the children from a religious cult who wants to kill them?

Enduring Service (Book #3)

Amazon Top 100 Bestseller

978–0–9914034–0–0 (ebook)

978–0–9914034–1–7 (paperback)

Available as an audio book.

Colony Agent Sulie Metcalf, the President's private physician, has been in love with the same human man for nearly thirty years. She refuses to allow herself the joy of true love because her feelings are unrequited by her human boss, Jonathan Dixon. As Dixon's retirement looms near, and his memories of Sulie and the last thirty years of his life are about to be erased, does she confront her fear of intimacy and take a leap of faith before it's too late?

Dixon has decided to retire and enjoy what time he has left. When his best friend Sulie, a vampire team member, is kidnapped during a medical emergency, Dixon realizes that retirement means giving up everything, and everyone, he's known for the last three decades. Will he risk his life, and his heart, to save her?

Equality of Service (Book #4)

978–1–948997–07–2 (MOBI)

978–1–948997–08–9 (ePub)

978–1–948997–09–6 (paperback)

Available as an audio book.

Fifteen years ago, COLONY Agent William Wardell met his

future wife Jackie Pearlman. She's sexy, opinionated, and finds him to be a mockery of the American dream of equality for all.

Can a past Freedom Rider and racial activist from the 1960s, now turned vampire, prove to the love of his life that he's not a political puppet?

Reliant Service (Book #5)

978–0–9914034–2–4 (ebook)

978–0–9914034–3–1 (paperback)

Available as an audio book.

After faking his death from an assassination attempt on the President, and retiring his first and only alias with the COLONY, Daniel Brighton discovers the mandatory sabbatical to be less than exciting. He chooses to do a favor and act as a security guard for a fading pop–singer, Lori Austin, whose career is winding down. He travels across Europe with her and discovers her past to be one of deception and intrigue with a history leading directly back to the COLONY itself.

Lori Austin is struggling to keep her career alive, and is willing to do what is necessary to save it. From bad press and scandalous stories, she travels across Europe on a relief tour to revitalize her career, but doesn't realize she is traveling with a vampire. Discovering a hidden family secret, she realizes that the one man who can save her is the handsome security guard she fought so hard not to hire.

BOOKS IN THE "COLONY WORLD" SERIES

These vampire romances feature vampires from the COLONY world, but these vampires do not work for the government.

Winter Wishes (Book #1)

ISBN: 978–0–9981866–0–3 (ebook)

ISBN: 978–0–9981866–1–0 (paperback)

Available as an audio book.

Sammy needs a holiday miracle. The Vampire Council is after him, he's falling in love with his best friend's mother–in–law, and there's artwork hanging on the wall that was stolen by the Nazis. Life is spiraling out of control for this Jewish vampire as he spends the Christmas holiday baking cookies and wrapping gifts for the needy.

Louise is busy with her charities and hosting her annual Christmas party. Putting a smile on her face proves difficult when her soon to be ex–husband arrives with a bimbo on his arm, her proposed divorce settlement is far from fair, and the sexy stranger she's starting to fall for believes she's a Nazi.

~

Destined Desire (Book #2)

ISBN: 978–1–948997–16–4 (EPub ebook)

ISBN: 978–1–948997–15–7 (MOBI ebook)

ISBN: 978–1–948997–17–1 (paperback)

Available as an audio book.

After a car accident nearly kills his immortal father, Alexander rushes to his father's side only to discover that his parents want him to marry and stay closer to home. He's already been down this path once before with a less than desirable outcome, so he refuses. He's steadfast in his decision until his parents threaten to financially cut him off and he's forced to approach the Vampire Council for a new marriage contract.

Dionora is enjoying her new job at the Vampire Council Marriage Office. The holidays take an exciting turn for her when she discovers the next match she does is for her ex–fiancé.

Revenge is sweet with this sensual romantic comedy.

CONTEMPORARY SWEET ROMANCE SHORT STORIES

Taking Chances

978–0–9966192–9–5 (ebook)

Available as an audio book.

Broken engagement, a disappointed father, an emotional mother, what else could a wounded soldier ask for? Tommy has no idea that his sweet nurse remembers him prior to his injuries. Always professional, Abby treats Tommy no differently because of their awkward past. Once the truth is out, what will become of their friendship and budding romance?

Christmas Joy

978–1–948997–18–8 (MOBI)

978–1–948997–19–5 (ePub)

978–1–948997–20–1 (Paperback)

Jake needs to clear out his father's old cabin and sell it. He's prepared to deal with the freezing cold weather and the remote location, but not with the sexy woman, who was once his late father's nurse, still living in the place.

~

More Than Puppy Love

978–1–948997–01–0 (MOBI)

978–1–948997–02–7 (ePub)

978–1–948997–03–4 (Paperback)

Ex-wallflower, now veterinarian, Kacie Preston is eager to go to her ten-year high school reunion where she can meet up with the boy she crushed on for years. But then his dog, her patient, shows up at the event mistreated. How well does Kacie really know her old heart throb?

www.ingramcontent.com/pod-product-compliance
Lightning Source LLC
Chambersburg PA
CBHW030258130626
46549CB00002B/590